Wanda Domes

ROCKING

ROCKING

ROSALIND WRIGHT

HARPER & ROW, PUBLISHERS
New York, Evanston,
San Francisco, London

FIRST EDITION

Designed by Janice Stern

Library of Congress Cataloging in Publication Data

Wright, Rosalind.
  Rocking
  I. Title.
PZ4.W95167Ro [PS3573.R539]   813'.5'4   74–15897
ISBN 0–06–014752–0

75 76 77 78 79 10 9 8 7 6 5 4 3 2 1

To my mother and father with greatest love,
and to Amram Shapiro

I would like to acknowledge and thank:

The Quitman Nursing Home for opening their home and themselves to me, a hospitality which aided me endlessly in writing this novel.

Santha Rama Rau, my teacher, for her belief, guidance, and friendship.

Kathleen and Larry, Larry and Roberta.

R. W.

CHAPTER 1

From the corner of a small gray end table, a plastic squirrel peers from the shade of an ivy plant. Unblinking, he watches the man sleep. The walls of the room, some time ago painted a diluted yellow, are beginning to glow with the light of morning. There are curtains on the short double windows, but they are of thin material, translucent when an opened peony appears in the print. The floor is clean. Two pairs of black oxfords are arranged by the table. On a limed oak dresser across the room, a round clock ticks past seven. A few years ago the moment would have been exploded in shrill alarm, but this morning the luminous hand moves on with a single beat.

Ira Snow sleeps in bed 4C of the Twilight Days Rest Home. He wears tan pajamas. One hand is slipped under his pillow, warmed by the slight weight of his head. His white, slender legs are bent into a loose curl, covered by a sheet and a cotton spread. White toes flex momentarily in sleep. Behind folded eyelids, his eyes, Lancaster blue, move through a familiar dream.

In the neighboring bed, Henry Parker is about to wake

once more. Mr. Parker sleeps in fits, especially toward morning, when the weight of his fatigue is relieved, and the drowsiness, which would like to linger, finds the single bed cramped and still strange after a year's time. Mr. Parker coughs and one hand reaches up to rotate his round figure. He sighs uncomfortably as his bare chest encounters the metal edge of the bed.

Andrew Carlyle is awake in the first room of ward A. A quilt made by an unremembered woman still covers his body though the heat of the day is filling the room. He is tense; his thoughts are past the hour and the room, to a figure revealed by two open doors. Janie Lipscomb sleeps like a wounded rag doll, her shoulders propped against the back of her crib. One hand holds the hand of a pink air rabbit. The other is cradled in the familiar space between her sprawled and boneless legs.

Seven rooms away, Azzie Bowdin's staccato snores rise as she lifts her head from under a wool blanket. A chewed vinyl purse is clutched to her stomach. In the next bed, Miss Jimi June Hasbrook is deeply sleeping. A muslin gown with a smeared, illegible stamp across one breast has wrapped itself around her hips. Her thighs are slim and covered with soft, sandy, never-shaven hair.

"Igan wona por mah ecast, inna halertten, inna awuberi. Wak ema cally jinda. Jinda, jinda!" Dorothy Tyler turns on her radio to cover her roommate's running talk. Perry Como sings "Pennies from Heaven." Mrs. Fulbright, in a nearby room, strains to hear.

In the corridor Earl Brogdon is taking his first walk of the day. Breakfast does not begin until eight on Saturdays, but Earl starts his trek to the dining area much earlier, his minute steps forcing a tedious study of the dark white linoleum of the hall tiles, splattered at random with red and burnt umber. The same old white is on the walls and Earl inches by it, unsmiling. Mr. Hadley passes, nodding on his way to town.

"Good morning, Cranson. It's going to be a beautiful day. Look out that window. You can tell by the color of the leaves; not a speck of gray in them. I'm going to see about getting my toenails clipped today."

Vidy Phillips is sitting on the floor of the community room, merrily laughing at the dilemma of a cartoon cat. This room, the neighboring kitchen, and the eating area are slatted with the wood of local trees—red and silver maple, sycamore, oak, mimosa, and American elm—recalling the home of a five-cow dairy and alfalfa farmer. From the back door it is still farmland, beginning in a rolling sweep of Johnson grass and milkweed. It makes a pleasant view, especially in the green seasons and on those mornings when numbers of D. Byrd Case's famous breed choose to graze along the slope in thick clusters of black and white.

Downtown is four blocks away on a tar-topped, primitive road called Cullum Street. From the front porch in the summertime, the top windows of the orange neo-Georgian courthouse can be seen, and an oversize Lone Star, emphatically proclaiming India, Texas, to be the county seat. The name is of a strange and difficult land, but it was claimed once by a soldier passing through that the two places share a certain feeling in the hot months, as though plants and people's skin had been waxed, and muscles turned to water. It is dead summer of 1956. A Saturday. Only a few pickups have passed in front of the courthouse, where the confluence of highways is made to acknowledge the fact of India, in a maze of stop signs. Down 81 to Rose Hill, last night's three boarders at Terry's Motel are still rousing themselves. The Texaco and the Humble on the way to C. City are getting a slow start, and in the white frame farmhouses life is much the same as it is at Twilight Days. Breakfast is late, served and eaten while captivated by Mighty Mouse and Fury.

By nine-thirty, Uncle Robert Goodley and Henry Parker have taken their places on the front porch as the official greeters. Saturday mornings and Sundays after church are special times at Twilight Days. The community room is deserted, and all but the barest conversation has ceased. Residents sit alone in their rooms, their pants and blouses carefully closed, their faces alive with private anticipation.

"Come in!" Marsh Colloway beckoned.

"Hello," smiled a large woman in a pale summer dress that dug double rings into her opulent arms. "I am Sister Willamena, and this"—she gestured behind her, still smiling, to a quiet woman with a plain flat face and incongruously lovely blond hair, which she wore in a thick French twist on her neck—"is Sister Pauline. We are from the Calvary Class of the First Baptist Church."

"Yes," he agreed. "Come in. I am a member of the First Baptist Church of Alpy."

Sister Willamena smelled thick and sweet, like heavy fig jam. "Sit down," he insisted.

"You are from Alpy?" Sister Pauline asked, widening her mouth in a vague, hesitant way.

"Mother!" Marsh Colloway yelled at a small-boned

woman sitting on the far twin bed. "These women are from the Baptist Church!"

Elizabeth Colloway waved one hand in reply. "You don't say. Did you tell them . . . ?"

"Oh, yes, we're from Alpy," her husband affirmed. "My name is Colloway. Marsh Colloway, with two l's."

"And this is Mrs. Colloway?"

"Oh, yes. You ever been to Mount Peter? That's where she's from. They're adjoining communities, Alpy and Mount Peter." He raised his hands, slapping his palms together. "Right there, side by side. Alpy and Mount Peter."

Sister Willamena trained a sagging brassiere strap. "You don't say. You must have grown up together."

"That's right, we did."

"You don't say."

"What! What is she talking about?"

Marsh Colloway bent over his wife. "She wants to know if we knew each other when we were children! Yes, we did"—he returned to the church women—"being in adjoining communities like we were. I don't remember exactly when we met, it's been so long ago. We've been married since eighteen ninety-eight." He grinned. "Now, you figure that up."

Sister Pauline began to count on No-Color polished fingernails.

"Yes, ma'am. Fifty-eight years. That's no fly-by-night romance. No, ma'am. No whistle-in-the-wind affair. I don't know if she loves me or not, but we haven't fought the way some men and their wives do." He looked at Elizabeth Colloway with regard. "She's no bitch."

5

Sister Willamena exchanged a glance with her companion. "Do you have any children?" Sister Pauline inquired stiffly.

"One boy. And two grandchildren. That's right, isn't it, Mother? We have two grandchildren?"

"Of course, dear." Elizabeth Colloway raised her hand again.

"Our boy is still in Alpy," Marsh Colloway went on before he saw the man in his doorway. It was someone he did not know, a man with an overgrown flat-top, wearing a plaid bathrobe. "Hello," Marsh Colloway allowed. It was more curious than unfriendly.

"Hello to you," Emit Street returned gruffly, staring at the two visitors.

"These women are from the Baptist Church."

"Ah ha!" He nodded furiously. "I thought so. Just as I thought." He pointed to his bare feet. "I can't find my shoes. Somebody has taken my shoes."

"What a shame," Sister Pauline offered.

"It was you, wasn't it?" He gave her a searing look. "You took my shoes for your damn church! And I'm telling you one thing: I want them back!"

"No, I assure you," Sister Pauline protested in her small voice, but Mr. Street turned away. "People better leave my things alone," he warned from the hall. "There is going to be trouble."

"Perhaps you know our son?" Marsh Colloway injected immediately. "Herb Colloway at the Alpy Bank."

"No."

"No; I don't either," the women answered in hurried succession.

"He is a fine boy."

"I'm sure he is." Sister Willamena edged out of her armchair. "Mr. Colloway, Mrs. Colloway, we certainly have enjoyed our visit with you." She held out her hand and Sister Pauline gave her a tiny white Bible with gold print from a paper bag she was carrying. "We want you to have this little Bible as a gift from the Calvary Class."

"What is it?" Mrs. Colloway demanded suspiciously.

"It's a Bible, Mother! I'll take it. The print is too small for her to read," he explained. "But I will read it to her."

"You do that, Mr. Colloway. It is the Lord's book."

"Don't forget where we are, now," he called out. "We're always right here. The door's never locked."

Sister Willamena smiled again and moved on, stirring her scent.

Ira Snow heard the sound of them coming, sharp and narrow heels, and he turned toward the door, raising his brow to make his closed eyes obvious, and pushed out loud and regular breaths. "This one is sleeping," he heard the first say to the second, who wondered in a stage whisper why he would not cover himself or close his door if he wished to sleep. Nothing audible was replied.

Ira blinked. It was one or two hours after noon, a time when kicking the sheet off his leg felt to Ira like stepping out of a hot bath and suggested the weak sleep likely to follow. But he resisted. These were his favorite hours, when Henry Parker was busy on the front porch and the room was Ira's alone. He only wished to continue lying as he was now—his nose, mouth, and chin buried in the damp sheet, his small stomach tucked under his ribs. On Saturdays, he thought of Sarah constantly.

"Did you get a good look at Monica Whitwell, Henry?"

"Put on a little weight, I thought."

"I should say. Did you notice that, Cranson?" Uncle Robert addressed the empty chair next to him. "Of course, her father is so hard on her, I don't blame the poor girl for eating a bit too much cake."

"Adam means well." Mr. Parker stretched out his long legs. "Besides, I never minded a little fat on a woman."

"No, neither did I," Uncle Robert agreed. "It's Cranson here. He likes them skinny as a toothpick."

Henry Parker surveyed the parking lot and the street beyond. "Looks like that's about all the visitors for today."

Ira closed his eyes. "I'm seven," Sarah told him, her coal eyes darting about, nervous and friendly, while her incredibly boned back shivered with a gust of November wind. "I am going to live next door with my mother."

CHAPTER 2

Monday

Dearest Phillip,

I know I usually give the time of my letters, but I seem to have lost track of my watch and there is no way of telling without it. If you were here, you could read the sun—I have a glimpse of it through a long window in my new room. A woman came a while ago with some lunch. How long? An hour? Three? I am so bad at these things. That would make it two if lunch were early, four at the latest. Though it might have been only one hour instead of three. I could only take a bite of bread. I am without my famous appetite these days.

This room is enormous. There is a fine old bed with fresh towels laid across the headboard, a chair by the window (one of my favorite things), and a ridiculously large dresser which I will not begin to fill because I intend to leave all of my winter clothes packed, and will not disturb your trunk. Not all of the motel is like this. The woman who showed me to my room told me that this is by far the largest room. It was meant to be something else, a lounge or something on that order, and then someone fell ill and plans changed—a long story. But Jamie was right, this is a much nicer motel than the Alamo Courts. You remember Jamie, my cousin from Allenwood. I don't know how long it had been since I had

9

*seen Jamie. Suddenly he appeared at the Alamo. How he found me—
but surely I have written you all of this. He claimed to have heard
disreputable things and no cousin of his, etc. Such a state. I tried to
assure him that I was quite comfortable there, especially for such a short
time, but he would not hear of it. This morning he moved me part and
parcel to India, a tiny town which Jamie says is about thirty miles east
of C. City. I will find out the exact directions and include them in my
next letter.*

*Remember those pictures Beth Walters had in her living room? Two
relatives hang above my bed—the only drawback to a fine room. I love
you.*

Katy

*P.S. I completely forgot—the name of the motel is Twilight Days, on the
edge of town. I am in room 25B. I can't wait to see you again—
K.*

Kathleen Storrs was not expecting company on her
first day. She undid her best dress, wintergreen with
white stripes, and slipped on a beige flannel nightgown,
worn into being cool enough for summer. The dress she
hung by itself in a narrow closet, built where the room
took a sharp turn with the building. Everything seemed
put away. She caught sight of herself in the bureau mirror. Kathleen had always been pretty, fine ecru skin, but
it no longer concerned her. It mattered only that she
look familiar. She smiled now at recognizable alexan-
drite eyes. She was similar if not the same as when Phillip
had left. Physically, her mood seemed more . . .

She had daydreamed and forgotten what she was
about. Kathleen removed a gold box from her dresser;
it was embellished with macaroni shells and her maiden
initials. Inside were many blue envelopes. She sealed the

day's letter in one and added it to a collection of identical letters kept in a drawer of their own. At the end of every week she tied the letters in groups of seven, with ribbons made from shredding an old pale blouse. Kathleen had not had her husband's address for some time, but binding them was a neat task that gave her pleasure, and so she would continue, every Friday afternoon, until she heard from Phillip.

"I used to smoke," Henry Parker grumbled and pressed a spoonful of boiled white potatoes into his mouth. "When I was a youngster, I started. Just a cigarette or two. And of course down at the Crystal we all smoked, but Martha Helen never would let me bring it into the house. Said it would kill the cat." Mr. Parker waved his fork. "But I'll tell you, Ira, one day that old cat got run over, and I went out and bought myself a pipe. Imported, as I recall."

"You have to be young like that," Ira indicated with a nod. "You have to have a young system to digest all that smoke. Wouldn't be good for you now."

"Humph," Mr. Parker conceded, softening the potato with his tongue. "He's still got a few more years before he will have to give it up."

"Yes. Indeed. Did you see him today?"

"No. Next Tuesday."

"He seems to be a fine doctor."

"I don't know about that." Mr. Parker pushed his plate away. "He's such a kid. I don't see why he doesn't tell them to give us better food. One more meal like this and the ship will sink."

"I heard meat loaf for dinner."

"Remember those potatoes Martha Helen used to make? Do you remember those, Ira? You were there a few times when she made those potatoes. Onions and cream poured all over the top. Cheese." He shook his head.

"She was quite a cook," Ira agreed.

"Yes, she was. And a woman. I was married to her for forty-six years." Mr. Parker raised his shoulders. The loose skin from his plump elbows folded on the table in spotted layers.

"It's a crime, Ira. It's a crime to make a man live this way, on this food, without a wife to make a proper supper for him. I would never do that to any man. I am almost old enough to be God, and I would never do that if I was."

Ira felt a quick tremor; he pressed his hands together. "If you were God, Henry, it wouldn't be men getting your attention."

He chuckled. "No, sir, Ira, I wouldn't change one fingernail on the ladies. Best leave well enough alone. What I always say."

"I heard there's a new woman here. Moved into Mr. Jaffie's room this morning."

"Oh? From town?" Mr. Parker picked up a bowl of custard from his tray.

"Jason saw her come in and said she was a stranger."

"Damn it all!" Mr. Parker threw down his spoon. "This is lemon! I've been sitting here the whole meal getting worked up for coconut. Filthy trick."

"You want my potatoes?"

"They aren't coconut, are they? No. What else did Jason say?"

"I'll take your custard if you don't want it." Ira reached for the bowl.

Mr. Parker caught his hand. "Did you ask the doctor about this?"

Ira tried to reclaim his hand. "It's just a chill, Henry. The door to the kitchen is open."

"What did he tell you?"

Ira smiled slowly. "He said it was a sign of my youthful exuberance."

"Ha!" Mr. Parker swung Ira's hand free. "Have the custard if you want. That will kill your youthful exuberance." He picked a piece of ice from his water glass and chewed on it. "She must have family around here, this woman."

"Perhaps."

Mr. Parker said nothing for a moment. "I think so." He slapped the table and stood up. "I can't stand the smell of this feast any longer. I'm going out to the porch. You want to come?"

His friend declined. The weather, Ira said, called for an afternoon nap.

Crowds were brought to the community room by the donation the past spring of a first-generation television set, which sat magnificently in the exact center of the room on a table covered with a handmade pink lace cloth. The mass enthusiasm created the need for strict rules forbidding loud talking and ensuring adherence to an established viewing schedule. These regulations were enforced by Mrs. Dorothy Tyler, eighty-seven, who sat in a cushioned rocker in the far right corner. The dark stain of an after-lunch chew trickled from her mouth unnoticed.

At twelve-thirty Miss Jimi June Hasbrook was seated in her customary chair awaiting the first segment of her favorite program, "As the World Turns." Vidy Phillips took a seat next to her just as the commercials began following the noon news.

"What are you doing?" Vidy inquired politely.

"Sewing on a quilt," Jimi June replied. "One of the aides give it to me. She couldn't do it. Stupid girl."

Vidy selected a brown-and-yellow square from Jimi June's lap. "Pretty."

"These damn scissors won't cut."

"Did you ever try sharpening them with a piece of glass?" Vidy suggested.

"What?" Jimi June turned and narrowed her armadillo eyes on Margot Zeagler. "Did you hear that?"

"No, I didn't. I'm terribly sorry." Miss Zeagler smoothed her black hair, arranged in spoolie curls. "I was watching the commercial. Silly commercial; I've seen it a dozen times."

"We used to run them over the neck of a bottle," Vidy explained. "Sharpen them up real good. Then we'd eat 'em." Her heavy brown tongue pushed out of her mouth and curled up.

"Did you catch that?"

Miss Zeagler nodded, a quirk of horror and fascination playing on her roughed lips. "She said she ate scissors."

"One time I ate a whole piece of glass," she continued. "Big brown piece." Vidy laughed merrily. "Passed right out. Wasn't that lucky?"

"The commercial's over," Jimi June informed her.

"I thought that was lucky."

"I told you to shut up!"

"I heard you," Vidy replied. She ripped the quilt square into even sections and began to clean her ears.

"Henry!" Uncle Robert Goodley smiled broadly, displaying a wide white, white set of dentures. "Come on out and join us. I was just telling the boys, Henry, that I have lived in India, Texas, all of my life. That's a long time."

"I swear." Dr. Whitwell spat out a grape seed with a wet cough. "That has been a time."

"Eighty-three years that is, Henry. Time enough to know this town and what she needs. Now, she's got a lot, I'm not saying that. Cafés and stores. A newspaper. A town has got to have a newspaper."

"Ira would agree with that. He built us a fine one."

"That's what this country was founded on!" Uncle Robert struck the arm of his chair. "Freedom to speak out and have yourself heard. And we've got that here in India."

"A railroad," Dr. Whitwell reminded.

"Yes, sir; got to be connected to other people. You can get along without water now; not many ships." Uncle Robert chucked a seed across the porch, where it lay glistening for a moment in the midday heat. "Good thing. There's not much water in East Texas. But you've got to have a factory." He raised his eyes in conviction. "Future depends on putting out something like ladies' dresses or automobile parts. Something the country will take notice of. Get India on the map."

Mr. Parker nodded agreeably.

"No." Emit Street lifted his compact one hundred and sixty-seven pounds an inch or two in the air and returned to the round-back steel chair in a slightly different position. "Nobody's ever coming back to India. Everybody's got to go to the cities and have their fling, and it's chaos there." He twisted his hands sadly. "Madness. Nobody is ever going to return. I heard it on the news today." His pale eyes scanned the distance to town. "Niggers have ruined the country. Nigger preachers. Nigger policemen. There's nothing left, you know. That nigger girl over in Tuscaloosa trying to get into college with white kids. I heard it on the news today."

"Did they say what the weather's going to do?"

"Hot."

"Emit's right." Dr. Whitwell rolled his wheelchair to the edge of the concrete. "India's missed her time. All our young men are marrying and going off, taking the pretty young girls with them. No one to run a factory now. We could have done it. But there is no one now."

Henry Parker nodded toward the street. "Here comes Jason."

"I'm surprised they let him go to town. He's been having that trouble in his leg."

"Seems to be walking all right, though."

"He'll make it," Dr. Whitwell concluded with authority.

Uncle Robert sucked ponderously on the last purple grape. "We can't survive in this day and age without a factory. Even the Communists have them."

"I can see your point," Mr. Parker seconded. "This is the time of the Industrial Revolution, the Scientific Age, and we've got to keep in step."

Emit Street thrust forward. "The Communists have already got the country! That's what the doctor and me been telling you for months. None of it matters—factories, my eye! The country's gone. India's gone. Gone to the niggers and the nigger-Communists." He knocked over a chair that stood in his path to the door. "Just thank the powers that be we won't be around to see the end."

Jason Hadley had hundreds of forked wrinkles. They lit up like a maze of smiles. "I made it," he affirmed to the porch group. "There was a moment there when I didn't think I was going to, but by God, I did." He started to settle in Emit Street's abandoned chair. "Oh, excuse me, Uncle Robert. Is Cranson sitting here?"

"Not today, Jason. Too hot for him."

"Anything going on in town?"

"Not much, Henry. I saw Jack Durbey down at the courthouse. Didn't have no news. I sure wished somebody would open up that Crystal Café so I could have someplace to sit besides under them courthouse elms." He fluttered his hand in front of his chest, futilely trying to raise some wind. "Too hot for that now."

"Yes, sir." Uncle Robert slid a finger behind his ear and found the tiny irritated chigger bite. "I can remember when every Saturday morning of my life was spent down at the Crystal, drinking bad coffee and spilling the world's business. You remember that, Henry?"

Mr. Parker laughed. "I sure do. I was there."

"So was I," the doctor echoed softly.

It was almost one-thirty, the hottest part of the day. "Yes, sir. Yes, sir." Sleepy eyes followed the movement in the parking lot, the slow walk of an old black cat going home.

CHAPTER 3

Azalea Bowdin stumbled to her feet. It was the chance she had been waiting for since lunch. She listened as the sharp heels of Ima Johnston, the administrator of Twilight Days, passed in front of her, turned to the left, and grew faint.

Azzie made her way into the abandoned office and set immediately and without emotion to the task at hand. Her eyes were idle and independent, one looking like the third eye of a cat lowered to veil a recent wound; her fingers moved expertly across the contents of the second drawer of the metal file cabinet. Deftly she counted three raised tabs: the heading, *B*, Woodrow Barker, and Toni Joe Boswell. Azzie never let herself be tempted by an ill-timed curiosity. She was fully aware that she had only a few uncertain moments in which to accomplish her mission, and she went straight for the heart of her file, bypassing a thin blue inconsequential sheet she had the first time taken by mistake, finding out later from a better-sighted source that it contained only a windy account of her admission to Twilight Days. She selected a tired index card that listed her prescriptions and past inoculations, and a folded bit of paper discussing a slight irregularity in her heartbeat.

Azzie slipped the bounty into her vinyl alligator-patterned purse and closed the cabinet. She was purposeless now and leaned heavily on her cane, shaking her great round head with self-satisfaction. "Well, hello there," she cried, catching sight of a nearby form as she stepped into the hallway.

Henrietta Newman was checking the height of her bouffant hairdo. "What were you doing in there, Azalea?" she asked.

"I don't believe I know you." Azzie smiled. "But then I might know you and not know it." She squinted furiously. "Oh, you're young."

"You know me, Azalea," Mrs. Newman replied and tugged at the waistband of her white uniform.

"I'm sure I do," Azzie returned. The question no longer held her interest. "I'm sure I do."

"Are you lost? What were you doing in Mrs. Johnston's office?"

"Yes! That's just right. I just wandered in here." She looked around blindly. "I don't even know where I am."

"Come on, I'll walk you home." Mrs. Newman wrapped her arm around Azzie's loose waist.

"Honey," Azzie said softly as they began their slow walk. "I had a question, a little problem, and I was thinking maybe you could help me."

"What's that?"

Azzie wet her lips and smiled. "You know, this is such a fine place. I really do think so. And you are so nice. What did you say your name was?"

"Newman. Henrietta Newman. I've worked here since this place opened. This new building, I mean. Wait a minute." She released Azzie, who swayed uncertainly. "I've lost one of my pins." She retrieved a large opened bobby pin from the floor.

"And a fine job you do, too," Azzie declared as the arm reclaimed her waist. "They don't appreciate you around here. That's what I have been thinking about." She squeezed Mrs. Newman's hand. "You're so nice and my room is so nice. There's only one thing bothering me." She lowered her head demurely. "How much longer am I going to have to live with that butt-face?"

"Azalea Bowdin!" Mrs. Newman stopped. "That's a terrible thing to call anyone, especially poor, pitiful Jimi June."

"Pitiful!" Azzie raised her milky eyes toward the ceiling. "I'm the pitiful one for having to live with that jackass."

"You really ought to watch your language. You might get in trouble talking that way. It doesn't sound very Christian."

"I am a Mormon." Azzie pursed her lips defiantly.

Henrietta Newman smiled. "I would keep that to myself, also," she advised and resumed their walk.

"Baby," Azzie whispered almost inaudibly. "That Jimi June is so bad. She spits on the floor."

Mrs. Newman hesitated for a moment or two. "You probably don't know this"—she offered the confidence close to Azzie's cheek—"but Jimi June has been in a hospital since she was a young woman. Very young. Now, if she does some things that don't seem quite right to you, you have to keep that in mind. Be a little tolerant."

Azzie had long ago secured the story on Jimi June. She ignored the interruption. "She's making my life miserable. You've got to find me somebody new."

"We just moved you last month."

Azzie stopped and pulled away, her pudgy knees quavering with the weight of independence. "I am so blind."

"Are your eyes bothering you again? I could see the doctor about increasing your eyedrops."

"Baby, I am so blind." Azzie studied her pink support socks curiously. "Nothing is going to help me. I am so blind I couldn't even tell if that was somebody new in Mr. Jaffie's room. Poor man, I felt terrible to hear about him."

"Yes, it is." Mrs. Newman steered the old woman ahead.

"I couldn't even tell if it was a man or a woman."

"A woman."

"Do I know her?"

"I doubt it. She is from Cambria."

A puzzled smile turned to her. "You say her name is Ambra? What's that—Mexican?"

"No." Henrietta Newman raised her voice. "I said she is from Cambria; that's in the next county. Her name is Kathleen. Kathleen Storrs, I believe. Here we are."

"Oh? Is this my room? That was a fast walk. They're going to get us for speeding."

"Do you want this?" Mrs. Newman picked up a heavy maroon sweater from the floor.

Azzie accepted the garment and studied it. "I should say," she said upon recognition. "You all keep it so damn cold in here, I have to wear it or freeze." Azzie stretched out on her bed, giving a gasp as her shoulders missed the pillow. "Hey!" she cried before Mrs. Newman could get away. "What are we having for dinner?"

"I saw some chicken livers defrosting in the kitchen."

"Chicken livers?" Azzie chuckled to herself. "Well, I haven't had a chicken liver in a good long time. I think I will go down to the dining room tonight."

Mrs. Newman agreed. "That's a good idea. There are plenty of nice old folks living here, if you will only take the time to get to know them. I'll tell them to hold your tray."

"You do that." Azzie smiled. She placed her triple-lensed glasses on the floor in preparation for a short nap. "I believe I will go and eat my chicken livers in the dining room."

Kathleen Storrs was not at dinner. Azzie sat at the first table, directly off the hall, impatiently tapping her cane in response to Margot Zeagler's soft-spoken attempts at conversation.

"You don't see anyone new, do you?" Azzie interrupted.

Miss Zeagler moistened her lips. "I haven't been here very long. Only four months. I'm afraid I am not very well acquainted."

"You have two good eyes, don't you?" Azzie accused. "Look around. Who's that big blob at the next table?"

Miss Zeagler turned to face him. "Mr. Parker, I believe, is his name."

"Henry Parker. That's not who I want. A woman. A new woman. Keep going. Who's Henry with?"

"Another man. White hair."

"What about the next table?"

Miss Zeagler reacted with a shy eagerness to this hint of a game. She leaned forward confidentially. "One of them I am sure is Dorothy Tyler."

"How many with her?" Azzie strained her eyes. "I see two."

"Three."

"Is one of them skinny with"—Azzie fluttered her hands above her head—"crazy hair?"

"Yes!" Miss Zeagler was impressed.

"Fronie MacDermott. She and Dorothy are a pair. Gambling, you know. I don't believe in that. Not anymore. I am a convert to Mormonism." She nodded proudly. "Who are the other two?"

"One of them is wearing a blue blouse."

"No help."

Miss Zeagler wound a finger inside one of her tight curls. "She has gray hair. Straight and . . ." She hesitated.

"Becky Springer," Azzie pronounced. "Don't bother with the other one. Big bazooms, right?"

"Bazooms?"

"Breasts! Bust. Big bust, right?"

She nodded. "You could say that."

"Ha! I thought so. My eyes weren't always this bad. Go on."

Margot Zeagler described two more women in the corner and one who sat alone and appeared to be sleeping. Azzie assigned identities to them all. "Are you sure that's all there is?"

"I don't see any more. Although," Miss Zeagler added modestly, "I might be overlooking someone."

Azzie reached for Miss Zeagler's plate. "How can you overlook someone with usable eyes in your head?" She swept a half dozen untouched chicken livers into her purse and returned to her room.

Tuesday was the regular bath day for ward B. At nine-fifteen Earl Brogdon inched out of his doorway. Dr. Whitwell rolled down the hall in his wheelchair, followed by Uncle Robert, who giggled to himself. Emit Street ran his moist hand along the wall as he walked. An aide helped the wheezing Mrs. Fulbright; Dorothy Tyler hurried. "Nobody better dare touch me again while I'm on the toilet," she warned. The lanky Woodrow Barker slowed down to talk with Earl, and they all eventually filed by Azzie Bowdin, who had positioned herself at the head of the hall, directly opposite the oversize bathroom.

Bathing a ward requires three hours on best days— undressing, bathing, applying salve to bedsores and lotion to rashes, and putting pajamas and dresses back on warmed bodies. At various points in these proceedings, Azzie dropped her head for a cat nap, rousing herself frequently when the low rumble coming from the bathroom rose into momentary intelligibility. She listened for an unfamiliar voice, but there was none and at twelve-thirty the last bather emerged, pink and dazed from the hot tub.

Azzie threw off the remnants of sleep with a stern sideways shaking. What sort of woman was this, Azzie demanded, who didn't eat and didn't bathe? Perhaps it was all not true; it could have been anyone or anything in Mr. Jaffie's room. A coat hung on a rack, a patient curious about the smell of a room after death. But someone, Azzie could not remember who, had given her a name and a place: Kathleen Storrs from Cambria. Perhaps someone had played Azzie for a fool, yet it was impossible to detect the humor or purpose in an imaginary patient with a full name. Yet no one else had spoken of her. Miss Zeagler had not.

Of course! Azzie slapped the chair. The new woman had been forgotten. It would be easy enough for the fact of her existence to slip the mind of the one person who knew of her, probably one of those silly mindless girls who come around with their high voices, pushing magazines. In which case Kathleen Storrs might have been left for several days. She might be ill, even deathly ill by this time, and too weak to summon anyone. Azzie sprang to her feet, forgetting for once her state of precarious balance with the world, and hurried to the last part of the ward, where the building took a turn: 25B.

"Hello!" Azzie beat on the door with her cane. "Hello!"

Kathleen dropped a handful of cold water back into a glass bowl.

"Hello!" Azzie beat more frantically.

"Who is it? Yes?"

"I am your neighbor! Are you ill?"

Kathleen pushed her small breasts into her cotton dress and closed it hurriedly.

"I am your neighbor," Azzie's strident voice insisted. "Are you ill?"

"No."

Azzie's hand played more seriously with the knob and she leaned forward; her thick body careened into the room. "I had to make sure you were all right." She squeezed her eyes tightly closed and swayed back and forth. "I am blind."

Kathleen caught her as she rocked forward. "Sit down here. Please." She guided Azzie to the bed. "I will call someone."

Azzie arranged herself comfortably before cracking open her less clouded eye. Kathleen Storrs was not crippled, Azzie determined by the way the woman moved around her, but her hair was too radiant to be blond, and the hand rubbing Azzie's wrist was discolored by large tan liver spots. "I'll be fine," Azzie declared. "Just let me sit here for a few more minutes and get my bearings." She raised her other eye in a completely triumphant smile. "I am Azalea Bowdin. Azzie to you and a few select others."

Kathleen backed away shyly. "I am Mrs. Storrs." She perched nervously on her window chair.

"Yes!" Azzie agreed. "Kathleen Storrs from Cambria. I thought perhaps we knew each other. I have been to Cambria many times."

"I don't believe so."

"Well, perhaps not. But I had a friend in Cambria and I have visited there on several occasions." She paused significantly. "I have been all over. I have been to Europe more than once. My husband was a salesman."

"Do you know what time it is?" Kathleen asked abruptly.

"I have been all over," Azzie continued. "I had a mink stole that I wore when we traveled. They know all of that." Her eyes pointed past the open door. "That is why they don't want me to leave. They want my money."

Talk of money distressed Kathleen. It was a matter Phillip always handled. "Is it very expensive here?" she asked.

"I never see a cent of my money!" Azzie replied hotly. "They take it all."

"Why don't you go to another motel?"

"Motel!" Azzie shook her head so furiously that her gray bun threatened to topple. "I've had enough of them. I've been to every one in the civilized world. Hotels, too. I am going to the hospital."

"Are you ill?" Kathleen surveyed her visitor with renewed concern.

"Wait a minute!" Azzie waved her hand for silence. "The Veterans Hospital," she exclaimed in a moment. "That's where I am going. You see, Kathy"—she positioned her head forward, intent—"I am a blind veteran. Or my husband was—a veteran, I mean, not blind—so it's as good as me. Harry S. Bowdin was his name. And I am going to this special hospital where they will operate on my eyes." She opened her arms in a gesture of simplicity. "And then I will be able to see. My daughter, Peggy, is coming to take me. You know Peggy, of course."

"No, I don't." Kathleen checked the buttons of her dark dress.

"I thought you did. She has been to Cambria many times."

"No."

"Oh, yes, she has."

Kathleen Storrs stood slowly. One hand rested on a chenille coverlet draped over the chair. "I meant that I do not know her. Are you feeling better?" She glanced around the room and added to herself, "It must be almost two o'clock by now."

"Yes, I am." Azzie smiled. "Thank you. You will have

to meet my daughter, Peggy, sometime. Peggy Poteat. Isn't that cute? That's her name. She married a French boy in Louisiana. The Poteats. They are totally French." Azzie brought out a dated photograph from the pocket of her skirt. "Peggy is a beautiful girl." She held it up. "She just turned fifty last month."

"She looks very nice."

"Do you have any children?"

"No." Kathleen shook her head.

"What was wrong? You or your husband? So often it's the husband in these affairs, but they always blame the wife."

"It was. . . . " Kathleen smoothed the pleats of her full skirt. "I think I had better call someone to help you back to your room."

She received a pleasant smile. Azzie remained seated. "I can make it," she said. "I feel much better. I have these spells off and on and I just have to sit down until they pass." Azzie settled back on the bed to convince Kathleen of her well-being and comfort. "They usually come on when I am upset. I have been concerned about you, Kathy. You didn't take your bath today."

Kathleen stepped back toward the window. "I was trying to wash, I tried to wash this morning," she began. "I was asked to wait until Wednesday, for Mrs. Gilbey. I don't understand at all. They say her family comes on Tuesdays and the bathroom is unusually crowded, something like that."

"That is correct," Azzie confirmed. "Every Tuesday the Gilbeys come, rain or shine."

"I would rather take my bath alone, I always have"— Kathleen gestured to the towel on her dresser—"but all

I have here is a small bowl to wash my face and hands."

"It's a cheap place," Azzie declared. Her legs were sticky with sweat and she parted them. "I wanted to warn you about that. And"—she nodded with the experience of seventeen months at Twilight Days—"some of the people here are crazy. Some of them, like my roommate, have been locked up almost all of their natural lives. In the state hospital."

"They let them out?"

"They send them here! It's just another loony bin, for the old ones. There's one woman here, hasn't had any sense from the day she was born. And that nut I have now." Azzie rolled her milky eyes. "I'm going to get rid of her." She grinned shyly. "I want you to come and live with me. We would get along. You need the company."

"But my husband is coming," Kathleen protested quickly. "We will be going back to Cambria."

Azzie raised herself a few inches from the bed. "I had no idea you had a live husband."

"Oh, yes." Kathleen nodded. "He is away on a trip, but I expect him anytime. What is today?"

"Tuesday."

"Perhaps Thursday."

"And you will be going home with him?"

"Yes, certainly."

Azzie considered this. "All right," she agreed. "I will be going to the Veterans Hospital soon. You can move in with me until then. It's just down the hall." She gestured. "The next ward. At least I will be rid of that idiot Jimi June."

"But I have just moved," Kathleen explained. "I am all arranged here. I've written my husband where I am. I must stay here. Really I must."

Azzie stared at her for a long moment. "You should not worry people so, Kathy." Azzie stood with a great rocking motion. "It is not good for you to hide in your room. Skip baths. Everyone was worried about you; that's the only reason I came." She blinked her eyes rapidly as a reminder of their condition. "They asked me to come."

"I am sorry if I worried anyone."

Azzie hit the floor with her cane on every step. "You did," she replied, her back to the room.

Kathleen waited a few moments before closing her door. She straightened the bed where Azzie had been, and spent the afternoon lying down, only sporadically dozing. Around five she wrote to Phillip, asking him to come as soon as it was possible.

CHAPTER 4

Vidy Phillips went crazy at the age of thirty-one. If Joseph Phillips were still alive he would tell the story himself, especially if it were around five o'clock and a glass of beer were involved. It had seemed like a sudden thing at the time, he would confide, leaning back in his chair so that only the two back legs supported him, but after years of reflection he had concluded that there had been signs all along.

Vidy was beautiful, seventeen when he met her, and very much left to herself because of a wildness attributed to small-town beauties that alluded to self-celebration and vain freedom. Vidy suffered from this mythology and was lonely. She had no mother; four farmers comprised her father and brothers, and they had little business that included Vidy. In fact, it could be said with little exaggeration that by the time Joseph Phillips came through Whiston Mills, no one had talked to Vidy since she was nine or ten, other than to ask for a meal or to inquire about her health if she had a cold.

She overwhelmed Joseph with her response to his appearance in her life. Each time he came she would meet him far down the road, eager to tell him everything she had been thinking since they had seen each other last. The talk sounded strange and delightful on her lips, and toward the end of every sentence a small self-conscious giggle would escape. Joseph did not understand this excitement for confidences and friendship; at twenty-four, long-held secrets and bits of humor stale with years were not what he wanted from this black-eyed blooming girl. He did, however, understand about propriety and a woman's fear of scorn, and putting Vidy's giddy naïveté in those terms, he married her.

Joseph would never admit that his bride was a disappointment to him—his privacy was bound up with a complicated pride and an innate distaste for vulgarity. Vidy never refused him, but neither did she unleash the passion Joseph had imagined swelling beneath her exuberance. She followed him, responding to every guidance and command, but she was tender only, and without a sound. When he was done she would lie quietly and let him sleep, but on those occasions when a dream or a noise woke him later in the night, he often found his wife in the kitchen, making small sweets for his lunch.

It all began with the children, Joseph would contend, or more exactly with her first pregnancy. Vidy was very big with Steven and her size seemed to bewilder her; even after the birth she would stand in front of the mirror with her blouse pulled up, rubbing her hands over and over her stomach until she had left red scratches in her skin. She was restless with the child, prying him from her breast before he had taken his fill. When Joseph saw this and demanded that his son be well fed, Vidy re-opened her dress without complaint, but she held Steven loosely and without affection.

Joseph needed at least two sons to work the farm in Waketon as it expanded, and Vidy never said she was against another child. Indeed, the pregnancy seemed to calm her. She began to handle Steven with patience and some care, and by the time the baby was born, Joseph was ready to attribute Vidy's earlier skittishness to her own youth and a mother's exaggerated uneasiness with her first child. But Troy Daniel was barely a year old when Vidy went out and bought double locks for all the doors, to each of the five rooms and to the outside. She no longer wanted people coming to the farmhouse.

It was an outrageous request, which gave Joseph cause to rant against the tangents of women and most especially his wife. But Vidy was determined, and when people would stop by the farm, friends of his from town or even neighboring women who came by in the afternoon for a chat, Vidy would shout at them from a window or the door, then rush to the bedroom and close herself in, alone.

One Friday Joseph came home and found the bedroom locked. Knowing that someone must have come by earlier in the day, he banged on the door. "It's me!" he declared. "You can open this door now." Vidy did not reply, and his pounding did nothing against his wife's new brass locks. The sound of the baby crying could soon be heard throughout the house, but the door remained closed until Monday morning, when Vidy finally emerged, pale from not eating. Joseph was confused, but Vidy pierced all conversation with her stare, sullen and tense. A few days later he came upon two farm dogs dead from no apparent cause, and Joseph became fearful for his life and for his children. By the twenty-second of May, one week after Vidy had barred him from his room, he had the commitment papers signed by an understanding judge.

Vidy spent the next forty-nine years in a corner room in Fulton Hall, one of the original red brick buildings on the south side of the state hospital grounds. Joseph Phillips visited his wife only once during this time, and then only at the insistence of the ward doctor, who wanted to test Vidy's level of hostility after a series of shock treatments. Joseph stooped with apprehension as he approached her, but Vidy gave no sign that she suddenly remembered the spreadless bed she had come to loathe or the children this man had brought on her. She greeted Joseph as she did all intruders into her corner space, with a cold-faced and precisely aimed spit.

Vidy took no interest in crafts, she complained on walks, she had no ears for the gossip of the ward. When it was learned that she had been a regular in the Baptist choir, first in Whiston Mills and later in Waketon, a chaplain was sent to her room, but he made a quick retreat, the timid recipient of Vidy's hello. Vidy was soon left to the solitude of her corner, where she sat on the bed or in a brown chair, her energy devoted to working her tongue around her mouth, sucking and rolling it around until it became too thick and swollen to lie flat in her mouth; she let it droop to her chin or bathed the end of her nose.

By the beginning of the Second World War, Vidy was such a fixture in Fulton Hall that it was almost by chance that her improvement was finally recognized. One evening in 1943, a new nurse who was uninformed of Vidy's habits brought the evening tray directly to Vidy instead of leaving it on a table positioned at a discreet distance. Vidy thanked her politely for the supper, and when she returned to collect the tray Vidy shyly informed her that she had indeed enjoyed the lima beans. The young woman, just a month over twenty, was charmed by Vidy's friendliness and wet smile, and asked Vidy if she would like to take a short stroll down the corridor. Vidy consented and spent every evening of her remaining years at the hospital sitting on a bench in front of the ward station, entertaining the nurses and aides with the jokes and philosophy she had tried on Joseph fifty years earlier. Vidy's memory, or her willingness to remember, gradually returned, and when coaxed by her new audience she would assume a high, singsong voice and melodically recite her entire repertoire of friends, relatives, and neighbors, beginning with Joseph and the children.

Around the time Ima Johnston bought Twilight Days and moved it to the larger building on Cullum Street, a committee of doctors at the state hospital concluded that menopause had long ago ironed out Vidy Phillips's hysteria and pronounced that she was no longer a menace to herself or the state. The consensus was that the time had come to retire Vidy to a nursing home and to admit a youthful and still passionate creature to her bed. Numerous attempts were made throughout the summer and into early October to secure the family's approval, but all letters were returned to the hospital unopened. Because there were so many applications for her bed, it was decided not to delay the transfer any longer, and so, on the eighteenth of November of 1955, in a new blue Buick, Vidy got her first look in forty-nine years at the world outside Fulton Hall. She was momentarily terrified of the great number of vehicles on the road, but soon she was playing a gleeful peekaboo with passing cars. "Things haven't changed much, have they?" she demanded from the floor of the back seat.

They took the route down Mary Street to the narrow dirt throughway which gradually petered out into a path by the back door of the hardware store. There were more trees on Mary than on other streets on the same side of town—at least they were bigger, being elms, and offered some shade—but still it was the hottest day he could remember, Mr. Parker remarked. Ira nodded and wiped his face and neck with a white handkerchief. He gestured toward the wilted zinnias in a passing garden and the broken tan blades of grass paralyzed in midseason. "Summer has killed everything."

"It's about to kill me," Henry Parker replied, frowning at the gray dust riding his shoes. "The tar on the damn streets is melting, look at that. Pretty soon you won't be able to walk on these roads."

Mr. Parker preferred the late fall and winter, when wind and rain banished all dirt and smells. He preferred the anonymity of walking that time of year. Not like July, when his shoes squeaked with the sweat that pooled inside.

"I'm going to get a shoeshine," he told Ira.

"Yes," Ira agreed, thinking that shined shoes would do wonders for his friend's mood. Ira enjoyed his trips to town with Henry; he felt a remote sense of homecoming as they rounded the side of the hardware store and came upon the center square. The courthouse was a cumbersome bit of architecture to sit in the middle of things, Ira decided, looking at it, and the tiny dome perched above three wide stories lent the dignity of a gaudy party hat. But even at that it was a familiar landmark and Ira greeted it now with tolerant affection.

The paint job on the newspaper office had been completed since Ira had last been to town; the new light beige erased his name, but Ira noted with pleasure that the entranceway had been left alone. The double glass doors still surveyed every visitor with a cool glance.

"You want to stop for a minute?" Mr. Parker asked, nodding toward the courthouse benches.

"I think it's too hot for that, don't you, Henry?"

"I suppose. India looks dirty today, doesn't she?"

Carl Davis was cleaning his razor when Mr. Parker and Ira reached the barbershop, on the far side of the square.

"Hello, Henry." Mr. Davis waved a long razor. "I didn't know whether you would come in this hot weather. Quite a walk."

"I swear it is," Henry Parker replied and fell into a chair near the fan. "Where is Elton?"

"Gone for a sandwich. He didn't take the car, so he must have just gone down to the Dairy Bar."

"I'll wait." Mr. Parker stretched out in his seat, opening his arms and legs to the whirling breeze. Ira flipped through an April issue of *Boys' Life.*

"We've give up eating at the drugstore, Elton and I," Carl Davis explained. "It's just not the same with Firecat gone. He used to make chicken hash, fried in little patties like hamburger, and give it to you on some toast. I never tasted the like, and I suppose I never will again. You know how he came by that name, I guess."

Ira shook his head.

"Well." Carl Davis sat on the arm of a chair, savoring the prospect of telling a story. "This has been quite a while ago, but let me see if I can remember it right. He came down to the Texaco one afternoon—his name was John Paul then—and he and Nick really got into a spiff. Nicky claims old John Paul said things he ain't never heard come out of a nigger's mouth, but I don't know. I think maybe he had his reasons. They were charging him something like ten, fifteen dollars to fix a flat on his car. He was the first of his kind to have a car around here, you know. Anyway, it didn't set well with Nick at all, none of it, and he got some of his friends together and they followed John Paul home that night. They waited until he'd had time to get to sleep, and then they set that shack on fire but good. Well, you both know Nicky. They all went sauntering home, bragging that they had taken care of one nigger, and who should come in the gas station the next morning and buy a pack of Juicy Fruit with a five-dollar bill? That old dead nigger. Nick said it was the five dollars that really got to him. Anyways, nobody ever called old John Paul anything but Firecat from that day on."

"Anybody around to do a shoeshine?" Mr. Parker asked abruptly.

"Mrs. Pascal's son was in here the other day looking to do some odds and ends for extra money. He wants to go on that Boy Scout Jamboree next year. I think Merrit put him to work helping with the inventory. I'll call next door to the hardware store."

"You know the Pascals got a divorce, don't you?" Henry Parker turned to Ira. "I think I heard he's already married somebody else." He pulled at the white hair on his arm absently. "I'm not sure about that, though."

Five minutes later Larry Pascal banged through the door carrying an oversized steel tackle box. Carl Davis pointed to Mr. Parker. "There's your customer."

The boy took a seat on the floor in front of Henry Parker and with great importance examined the five containers in the makeshift shoeshine box. "What color do you want?" he asked Mr. Parker.

"Some sort of black," he answered and reached for the two tins that the boy held out. "Let me see. I think midnight is the darkest, don't you, Ira? Wouldn't you say that midnight is darker than jet black?"

Ira considered it. "Midnight might have some blue in it." He smiled at the blond boy sitting cross-legged on the floor. "Did you say your name was Larry?"

"Yes, sir." He scooped out a sizable amount of polish with a stained cotton cloth.

"How old are you, Larry?"

"Nine."

"My goodness." Ira laughed, leaning forward. "I know a little girl but she is only seven. Much younger than you."

"Yes, sir. I am in the fourth grade."

Ira nodded solemnly. "She is only in the second."

"My sister is in the second."

"Perhaps your sister knows her," Ira suggested. "Her name is Sarah Aberdeen."

"Sarah Aberdeen?" Henry Parker interrupted irritably. "Is that the little child you used to be so fond of? I thought she moved."

"Yes, she did," Ira answered, "but I thought Larry's sister might remember her." He turned hopefully to the boy. "Pretty little girl with long black hair about the color of that shoe polish there."

Larry shook his head, hesitantly applying a rough brush to Mr. Parker's oxfords. "I don't think so. She's never been around with Joseann."

"Well." Ira settled back in his chair. "I suppose you are not very interested in little girls yet."

"Where did the little girl move?" Mr. Parker demanded.

"Illinois. Peckenaw, Illinois. It's a little town."

"Illinois! Then why in the Sam Hill are you bothering this young man about her? That's been years, Ira." Henry Parker was provoked by Elton's long lunch and the mindless prattle, which was unlike Ira. "That's enough, Larry." He counted out fifteen cents in nickels and pennies. "Nobody will ever know I even had a shine by the time I get home." He glanced around irritably. "Where the hell is Elton?"—who followed the question almost to the punctuation. He was accompanied by a pleasant-looking man in his early fifties who remembered Henry from his days with the bank.

Max Churcher picked a dried piece of blood from a welt on his stomach. It had formed just while he was sleeping. It made an insignificant crunch in his mouth. There seemed to be little blood left in his belly.

He scratched but his fingernails were nothing; it felt

like stroking and provided no relief. He rolled onto his side and pushed his body up and down against the steel edge of the bed. Like a dog in the summertime.

"Where is my shot!" he cried. Earl Brogdon turned over in the next bed.

"My shot!"

Henrietta Newman appeared in the doorway. "What are you saying?"

"My shot. I need my shot."

"Mr. Churcher." Mrs. Newman pulled at her uniform. "You just had lunch. Don't you remember? You're not due for a shot until four o'clock."

He raised his gaunt body on one elbow. "Would you kill me?"

"It won't do to have you shouting like this."

"Get my shot!"

"All right, Mr. Churcher," Henrietta Newman replied evenly. "Just this one time, and only because Mr. Brogdon needs his rest. Of course, you never think of him. And don't think for a minute that I won't tell the doctor about this." She disappeared from the doorway.

Max Churcher stared at his roommate. Earl Brogdon's eyes were tiny, creased, snakelike whether they were opened or closed. He was asleep or in pain most of the time lately, or so he told Mr. Churcher, who demanded to know why he was always squinting. Mr. Churcher suspected it was a coward's excuse to stay inside, to be left alone. He stared at Earl Brogdon's tumid sleeping ear.

Mrs. Newman returned carrying the slim brown case. Max Churcher rolled onto his belly. His back was a field of needle holes and sores. He thought nothing of how he looked to her as she raised his striped pajama top. He imagined the needle she was preparing, sharp, smooth, easy-sliding. The imperceptible gush of fluid.

"I'm going to have to give this to you in your arm, Mr. Churcher. Your back is still covered with that rash, and we're going to have to give these sores time to heal."

He slid effortlessly onto his back. He closed his eyes against the brightness streaming in from a part in the curtains. Like a dog in the sunshine.

CHAPTER 5

"No, Cranson." Uncle Robert Goodley sat up in bed. "No. Now, I didn't leave that piece of candy there for you to eat. A bug climbed over it, a big black bug. A kind we've never seen before. You must not eat that piece. Here, I have some more." He opened the drawer of the uniform gray end table beside his bed. "Do you like orange? I don't like this one. But only one, Cranson. Lunch is only an hour away, and I know you. It's why I always lock up my valuable things. I know you, Cranson. I always have.

"What do you think about that kid beating old Archie? I'm telling you, I couldn't believe it." Uncle Robert unwrapped the foil from a cherry hard candy. "That Archie's got a right hook like a mule kick. I didn't think anybody could get by that. Course, he's old now, they don't say how old, but that Patterson's just a kid. Henry was pulling for him. I was down in the room there"— Uncle Robert gestured—"watching the game with Henry and Doc." He shook his head. "Doc's so busy now he hardly has time to talk. And yesterday Henry took Ira off to town. I really wish you would sit out on the porch with me on days like yesterday, Cranson." Uncle Robert raised his eyebrows and smiled. "It would be like old times.

"Do you remember Edna very well, Cranson? Probably not; you were pretty young when she died. She was always jealous of you, always after me to open the car door and let you out like a dog. As if you couldn't find your way home! I remember the time I went off and forgot you at that auction in Oklahoma City. What? That's right." Uncle Robert chuckled. "As if you would let me forget. Why, you were back home forty minutes after Edna and me, without benefit of automobile. Yes, sir, Cranson, you're some boy."

Jimi June walked with her shoulders thrust back as though she had great laborious breasts which threatened her with instability. In truth, her breasts were small pointed mounds that rode almost unnoticed high on her chest, but she was fiercely proud of them in the way of a woman pregnant a week. She asked more often than others that her dresses be washed, so that gradually the material thinned, forming a sheath like nylon across her chest (her nipples pushing out as she thought of this now). It was her most well-worn dress.

She passed Ira Snow in the hallway. She did not know his name and she thought of stopping him to ask, but it was a humid day and she stayed on her path to the Coke machine. She carried the last dime of her week's allowance; she would have no more money until Monday. Jimi June had no reserve to call for at the desk, as some did. She did not even know where her dollar a week came from, whether her sister sent it or the home provided it or whether it filtered down from some anonymous gift to charity. Nor did she care. It seemed like a paltry sum.

There was a long yellow sheet taped to the machine and she paused, her tongue darting across her lips in its anxiety of thirst, as she painstakingly read a memo panegyrizing milk and water and asking residents to limit their intake of carbonated beverages to one per day. There was a postscript, handwritten in red ink, requesting the staff to set an example.

Jimi June loved the sound of a dime running through the machine. It was shorter than the process required to count two nickels or to dole out the change from a quarter, but it was neater, sharper, and more Jimi June's style. She raised the metal door and laid her hands on the belly of a cold 7-Up bottle.

A man wearing a bright plaid shirt appeared around the corner. "Did you see this?" she asked.

Andrew Carlyle thrust two nickels into the coin slot and studiously avoided looking at the notice.

"It says we're not supposed to have but one of these a day." Jimi June gestured with her bottle, straining her breasts forward.

Andrew concentrated on opening his bottle.

"Do you think that is right?" she persisted.

"Nobody's going to tell me what to do," he barked. He usually took his afternoon Coke to the porch, but today he stood where he was, taking an extraordinary swallow, which produced a sizable belch.

Jimi June smiled with only the corners of her mouth, a hesitant grin in her eyes. "What's your name?" she asked.

"Carlyle."

"That's your name? Carlyle? People call you Carlyle?"

"Why do you want to know?"

Her drink was untouched. "I don't. I don't care. I'll call you Carlyle."

"Andrew Carlyle."

The smile reappeared, twitching in its eagerness to expand. "You're not new around here? I've seen you around."

"No."

"I've been here three years," Jimi June told him. "Almost longer than anybody. I was out at the other place, the one on the highway. Were you out there?"

"I came last fall."

"Yeah." Her squab hand toyed with her belt. "It's not too bad at this new place."

Andrew Carlyle gasped and drew in his breath, punctuating another belch. "I'm going to get out of here. I hate this place. I'd rather be sitting out the time in hell."

"Me, too. I'm going to get out, too. What did you say —hey!" She gasped and jumped back.

Andrew stepped with her, his fingers flexing quickly in and out on her right breast before he dropped his hand. "Go on now. I wasn't hurting you."

Jimi June crossed her thin arms over her chest, pulling her shoulders forward as though she were in pain. "What did you do that for?"

"I don't know." He turned away.

"What did you do that for?" There was a young whine in her voice, which stopped him.

"I wanted to," he replied, making his voice casual though unusually soft. "My wife's been dead."

"Oh, yeah?" Jimi June dropped her shield, intrigued. "I never had a husband." She took a sip of her 7-Up.

"Humph."

"Was your wife pretty?"

"I don't remember. It's been thirteen years." He walked around to the other side of the machine and dropped his bottle in the wire basket. "You're pretty not to have gotten married," he mumbled. Jimi June did not hear.

"You're the first one who ever did that."

He stared at her.

"Since I've been grown up anyhow. Once when I was a kid." She took another swig, bringing the level of liquid down to the top of the white 7. "Do you do that a lot?" she wondered. A long swallow: *You Like It. It Likes You.*

"Not lately."

Jimi June edged back her shoulders. "I suppose you get used to it."

"It becomes a habit." He was amused in spite of himself.

"Yeah." Jimi June nodded. "I don't like the other, though. My sister told me about it. It hurts."

"The other what?" Andrew demanded.

"You know."

"Oh." His voice was strange. "Yes, I suppose it might at that."

Jimi June studied him. "I've got to sit down," she declared. "I'm going back to my room."

"I'm going out to the porch," he replied, telling her for no reason he could understand.

Becky Springer sat in a chair by the window. She was

wearing a great pink flannel cap, her declaration of a cold coming on. She was idly watching the plants growing beneath her window: snapdragons, pansies, yellow roses, petunias growing furiously in spite of the heat, daisies, and two-tone marigolds, planted later by Mr. Hadley and still only sprouts. Becky spent every afternoon in this way, worrying over the threat of slugs and mockingbirds, and planning next spring's garden. She was terrifically irritated when disturbed in these deliberations, but this afternoon Vidy noticed that the garden catalogue lying in her lap was closed, and she seemed to be staring past her flowers.

"What are you doing?"

"Oh." Becky turned her head from side to side and rubbed her neck. "I'm thinking," she answered in her crow voice. "I've got to find somebody to write a letter for me. My sister-in-law died and I'm not sure her family knows about it. I don't know why I write them. They never write to me. Makes me so gall-blasted mad."

Vidy's tongue turned rapidly in her mouth. "They ought to write you," she agreed.

"Sure they should. Nobody writes me. The last I heard from that bunch was a Christmas card two years ago." She shrugged. "I don't know, maybe they're all dead. It's been so long since I've heard. They could all be dead and gone. I'll be the next. I wish you could write."

"I do, too. I sure would write them for you if I could."

Becky did not reply, and Vidy hurried on. "Did you see that book I got?" she asked.

"I saw that story book you had. You showed me that a hundred times."

"The Sunday school teacher give me this one." Vidy

pulled a paper coloring book from under her pillow. "It's full of animals, see." She knelt in front of Becky and slowly flipped the pages. "We had a little mew cat like that one time, and a piggy, too." She laughed merrily. "I done them all."

"Yeah, I can see you did."

Vidy quickly licked her lips four or five times. "But I didn't have no white crayon." She traced the smeared outlines of a black-colored princess on the last page. "I must have lost it, don't you reckon?"

"I suppose so." Becky cleared her throat in a hoarse cough. "The way you leave things around."

"I don't think they're as good, do you?"

"What are you talking about?"

"Do you know where they came from?" Vidy demanded. "Africa. Africa—one of them told me so herself. Down there with those little-bitty crawling things. We had one in our attic."

Becky absently joggled her heavy breasts. "Niggers? Is that what you mean? I wish you would say what you mean."

"Niggers!" Vidy pointed to her picture. "I don't think they're as good, do you? I have to get another picture. Do you figure they have them?"

"Oh, leave it alone," Becky commanded impatiently. "Niggers are all right as long as they keep away from you. They're just the same as anybody else, at least to me." She turned away to study her bush of sweetheart roses. The leaves were laced with the meals of small black bugs. "I just want everybody to leave me alone."

"Yeah." Vidy nodded. "I knew one once. Pauline. She went off somewhere. I never did see her again." She wet her chin and carefully replaced the book under her pillow. "I suppose if I call her Pauline, it will be okay."

"What do you need, Azalea? I haven't got much time today. I haven't got any time at all, if you want to know the truth."

Azzie smiled. "I want to write to Peggy."

"Peggy!" Bess Turner, the afternoon aide, shook her head, a wisp of her white-blond hair falling on her hot forehead. "We just wrote her a few days ago."

"Yes, I know. I want to write to her again." Azzie's smile was patient. "Are you that sweet woman who helped me home the other day?"

"No, I am not." Mrs. Turner arranged her plump thighs on the seat of the narrow vinyl chair, wincing as the rim cut into her leg. "It will have to be short; just a note. That's really all I have time for today. Where's your paper?"

Azzie pointed to the drawer of her end table. "You will have to get it for me. I can't see a thing." She pulled the photograph from her pocket. "This is Peggy."

"I've seen Peggy."

Azzie stared at her intently, trying to focus by tilting her head. "Yes," she replied and covered the picture with a slip of newspaper. "She was fifty last month. This is her address. She lives in Belle Vue, Louisiana. That's French. Her name is Poteat." Azzie grinned broadly. "French."

"Louisiana is a nice state," Mrs. Turner remarked, fixing the date, July nineteenth, in the upper corner of the pink-lined stationery. "I went there on my last vacation. 'Dear Peggy, It is very hot here and we need some rain.' "

"Yes!" Azzie was pleased and settled back in her chair. "That is good."

"What else?"

"Well." She was thoughtful. "I want to tell her that I am looking forward to her coming, and I hope it will not be too long until she is here." She touched the small bun perched precariously on the top of her head. "Did you see what that woman did to my hair?" she demanded. "She made me look like an old woman." Azzie snorted, "Course, I am one, but there's no law that says I have to look like it."

"You look fine, Azalea. I like the way Grace has done your hair."

"Did you tell Peggy that you are writing this letter for me?"

"Yes," Bess Turner lied. "Is there anything else more that you want to say?"

"When you come— Write this down. When you come, I am going to the hospital."

"All right. I've got that now."

"The Veterans Hospital," Azzie continued, "in— What's the name of that town?"

Mrs. Turner glanced up. "Where? In Louisiana? New Orleans?" she guessed. "Baton Rouge?"

"Yes!" Azzie exclaimed. "Baton Rouge. And then I will be able to see."

"Okay." Bess Turner finished the sentence. "I think that is enough for now."

Azzie felt in her lap for her glasses. "There was something else," she insisted. "I don't remember what." She was distracted by a passer-by in the hall. "Oh, there's that old—" she began but suddenly remembered. "Peggy, I met a woman here the other day from Cambria, where Mr. Roscoe lives now, the dealer friend of your late father. When you come, I shall go to the Veterans Hospital. . . . Be sure you have that part," she instructed Mrs. Turner. "I hope it is soon. I am counting on your coming soon."

"Here you go, Azalea. You go ahead and sign this. I've already put 'Love.' "

Azzie demurred. "Honey, I am so blind."

"You sign it every time," Mrs. Turner chided. "You know you do. Now come on. I've got to be about my business." She pointed to the closing, her fingers tipped in deep red polish, which Azzie could make out. "Right under the word 'Love.' "

Azzie accepted the pencil and, pinpointing the spot on the page, squeezed her eyes closed. "Azalea F. Bowdin," she traced from memory and then, as though she had just recalled who the letter was to, or perhaps to ensure that her identity was firmly established in the mind of Peggy Poteat, she added an open-eyed, shaky "Mother."

"Excuse me," Kathleen Storrs called to Mrs. Peterson, who was sitting in a chair directly across from Kathleen's room. "Do you know what time it is?"

Elberta Peterson trained her beady dark eyes on Kathleen. "Whak." She smiled softly. "Ona sopi doba, doba."

"I'm sorry," Kathleen replied and stepped closer. "I didn't hear you."

"Laly ev kawa pobes."

52

Kathleen straightened, confused. "Oh, excuse me, please," she repeated when she saw the man coming down the hall toward her. "Do you happen to know what time it is?"

Jason Hadley smiled amiably. "No, ma'am. I'm sorry, I don't. My old watch was supposed to last a lifetime, but it gave out a few years ago."

"Thank you anyway. Thank you very much." Kathleen turned to nod to Mrs. Peterson and stepped the few feet back into her room.

It was odd, she suddenly thought, leaning on her closed door, that a sick man should have been put in this narrow room instead of being sent to a hospital. But that was it, why there was green-printed wallpaper instead of paint, or something like that. Kathleen could not remember precisely what the woman's words had been, or even precisely who she was or when she had told Kathleen about her room. The sick man must be very poor, Kathleen thought, or rather have been. He was certainly not with her now.

She walked to the window and resettled herself in the chair. She had been trying to write to Phillip all afternoon, but nothing had come to mind. She was losing her way with letters, she thought, and let her eyes fall to her feet. They were long. They would be considered extraordinary for a woman if not so slender. Her black shoes accentuated their proportions. Pretty, but not right for summer.

None of which did anything to compose the letter she wanted to finish. She took a fresh sheet of blue stationery.

Dear Phillip:

It was difficult to write to someone, even a husband, Kathleen decided, if you have not seen him for some time. How to begin became a problem, especially without a clock, because, if you had it, you could always start off with the time of day.

Hello, my darling,

It is now two-thirty. Three hours ago I was eating a nice light lunch of boiled chicken and new potatoes and, let me think, it was only a little less than thirty minutes ago when a visitor knocked at my door, a stranger with the wrong room, but very pleasant about the whole thing. . . .

Kathleen could not picture her husband's face with any degree of exactitude. Gray-to-green eyes, somewhere in between, not having anything to do with how they changed with different light but entirely with her uncertainty. She had several photographs of him, one or two with color, which could freeze that iridescence into eyes that she could think of when writing to him. But the pictures were packed away with his belongings, and she wanted Phillip to find them just as they were when he left. They would be easier—

Of course! The directions—how could he come without the directions, and she had forgotten to send them. Or it seemed she had forgotten. Kathleen paused for a moment with her pencil to recall all the roads and turns and while she thought of the route her glance was caught by two stalky rhododendrons that had long ago been planted beneath her window. They were without the care of a watchful gardener and dying.

Dearest Phillip,

    I wonder if the mint growing outside the kitchen window is still alive —it worries me.

    I asked the woman who brings my tray, a terribly nice woman from, of all places, Rowlins, Georgia—do you remember that little town?— for directions to India (what a rambling sentence!), and she gave me quite thorough instructions. Highway 37 out of Jaksboro comes right through India. You will see a large reddish building with a flag just as you come into town—the post office, I believe. The street just after that building is Front Street. Make a right on Front and go three blocks until you see Cullum Street, where you take another right. The motel is at the very end of that street, behind a white brick church. It is only five blocks or so from the main part of town. I have quite memorized these directions so I am certain they are just as she gave them to me.

    Are you going to St. Louis this time? If you do, please call Paul Wickerhurst and his wife and see how they are liking it. I am certainly going to miss them when we get back to Cambria.

    I look for you every day. Remember the name of the motel is Twilight Days. I am your loving

                                                               Katy

CHAPTER 6

Still a child's face, Andrew Carlyle thought, watching Janie Lipscomb, who stood in his doorway. "Boom! Boom!" She fired at him with a stubby finger.

"Go on," he called. "Get out of here."

Janie hugged her giant pink air rabbit and rocked back onto her heels. She raised the corners of her inflated companion's towel dress to give Andrew a chance to admire a long curled tail. "Boom! Boom!" She smiled and moved on.

Janie was on her way to the community room, where Sunday school would begin at three-thirty, a half-hour gift every Friday afternoon from the Calvary Class of the First Baptist Church. The first visit to Twilight Days by a Calvarette had brought the report that Christ was going under just beyond the parking lot. The class had rallied with a map of the Holy Land, a set of used hymnals, and a weekly fund to provide refreshments.

"Hello, Janie," Sister Clyeda welcomed her. As four-time past president of the Calvarettes, Sister Clyeda had been unanimously elected to officiate at the backyard missionary Sunday school. She was going into her second year. "That's a pretty baby," she commented, making a small frown at the toy. "Isn't he a little young to be coming to class?"

Janie pointed to her mouth and waited.

"No, I don't have any gum. You don't need it in class anyway. Take a seat now, Janie. Perhaps next time you will leave Mr. Rabbit in your room."

"Boom!"

Vidy Phillips was sitting on the couch next to Mrs. Colloway. Elizabeth Colloway nodded deafly as Vidy explained how they had met once before, at the state fair. It was a hot day, Vidy could remember, and she had worn a polka dot dress while Mrs. Colloway, it seemed, was in pink. Marsh Colloway rested his head on the back of the couch. He folded his hands quietly in his lap.

"Sit right down here, Cranson. I'm glad you came today!" Uncle Robert slapped his knee. "You're going to hear some fine music. Sister!" he called to the plump Willamena, seated at the piano. "Do you know 'Faith of Our Fathers'?" He sang out, " *'Faith of our fathers, holy faith!'* We haven't sung that one in weeks."

"Sister." Margot Zeagler timidly raised her hand. "Could we sing 'What a Friend We Have in Jesus'?" She smiled slowly. "That is my favorite."

Dorothy Tyler assumed the seat left vacant for her in the corner rocker and Sister Clyeda began. "Good afternoon," she addressed the class, positioning herself directly in front of the television set in the center of the room. "If everyone has his place, we are ready to begin. You all remember that last week we talked about Paul and his missionary journeys? And this week I promised you that we would finish following Paul on his way around the ancient world."

"We have to sing first."

"Of course, Robert. We always sing. I just wanted to remind you of Paul so that you could be thinking of him. Now the girls and I will do our little theme song. Okay, girls?"

Sister Mary Holley came obediently to the front and linked arms with Sister Clyeda, while Willamena began a frilly overture. Sister Mary Holley was the composer, and she sang out with extraordinary vigor for her size.

> We are the babes of Jesus,
> Tenders of His flock by day.
> In our hearts we hold His promise,
> And our souls will never stray.
>
> All of you are lambs of Jesus!
> Baptized in His holy love.
> And someday you'll hear him calling,
> "Come, your new home waits above."

Sister Willamena swung right into "Just a Closer Walk with Thee," followed by "Rock of Ages." She carefully ended with a chorus of "What a Friend."

Dorothy Tyler strummed the arm of her chair in time with the music. "What's that song?" Jimi June asked.

"Willamena, Willamena!" Uncle Robert waved his hand furiously when the music stopped. "You promised you would do 'Faith of Our Fathers.' I asked you first."

Sister Clyeda unrolled a color-keyed map of the Middle East.

"You heard me, didn't you, Cranson?" Uncle Robert

demanded, addressing the chair beside him. "When we first came in I asked as nice as you please for 'Faith of Our Fathers.' "

"Do you remember, class, where Paul was when we left him last Friday? He was in Greece—you see this little pink section? He was in Athens, wasn't he, Margot?"

"Yes, ma'am." Miss Zeagler pulled a hair from her lips and self-consciously traced the outline of her coral lipstick.

"Now he is going from Athens to Corinth, right over here. That is where Paul sent some of his most famous letters."

Uncle Robert slammed his hymnal closed. "Some kind of Baptist meeting it is when there ain't no singing! Come on, Cranson."

She raised her voice over the sounds of his leaving. "Do any of you remember what Paul said to the Corinthians?"

"Love Christ," Jimi June answered. "He said to love Christ."

Sister Clyeda smiled. "Yes, he did, Jimi. And we do love Christ." The group murmured its assent. "I love Christ," Jimi June informed Dorothy Tyler, who continued to ignore her. Jimi June studied her quizzically. "What's your name?" she asked.

"Now, Paul made a promise to the Corinthians. He testified that he had seen the resurrected Christ and promised that through that miracle all of us will be saved."

"When we die." Vidy pointed to the ceiling and rolled her tongue. "When we die."

"Yes, Vidy, when we die or when the Kingdom comes.

59

Do you know what Paul said about that?" Sister Clyeda reached for her Bible. "He said . . . Let me see, it's right here somewhere."

"Sister! Don't let that idiot look at me like that!"

"Janie," the teacher scolded as the pink air rabbit made a cockeyed flight to the center of the room. "Calm down, Janie. You want to stay, don't you?"

Janie pointed to her mouth and shuffled her feet in a heavy dance.

"No. No gum now. And leave that toy where it is. Do any of you know what will happen when the Kingdom comes?"

"We will all be happy," Becky Springer cawed.

"We will," Sister Clyeda continued, "because all of our enemies will be dead."

"The Devil!"

"The Devil and his evilness." She nodded. "And we can help to wear down the Devil. I don't mean that Christ can't take care of the Devil all by Himself—He can, any-time He wants—but you and I can make the whole thing easier by not giving in to temptation. Because when we sin, it's like we are giving the Devil a big dose of vita-mins." She glanced down at her open Bible and con-cluded awkwardly, "It's just as Paul said: All things are lawful but not all things are helpful."

She surveyed the class. Dorothy Tyler was quietly doz-ing. Jimi June was whispering furiously to Janie Lip-scomb, who sat slumped in her chair, her eyes fixed lovingly on her rabbit, asleep on the carpet just out of her reach. Dr. Whitwell was reading a Baptist newsletter he had borrowed from Mary Holley. "I think that is enough for today," Sister Clyeda declared. "Let us all try to remember Paul and the news he brought to us. Now, Sister Mary Holley has made us some refreshments"— she indicated a platter of cheese-covered Ritz crackers— "and she will pass them around just as soon as we have had our prayer. I think she made enough so that everyone may have two. Now"—she smiled—"what do you want to pray for this afternoon?"

"Rain," Dr. Whitwell suggested dryly.

"You all remember, class, that we want to count our blessings before we make any requests. What do we have to be thankful for today?"

"Is this the prayer?" Elizabeth Colloway inquired.

"Yes!" Sister Willamena called out loudly.

"Then I want to thank God for my son."

Sister Clyeda agreed. "We are all thankful for our children. And our husbands and other loved ones. And what about this lovely room?" she asked. "Aren't we grateful to Ima Johnston for providing this lovely room so that we could all meet together like this?"

Vidy Phillips nodded her head emphatically. "Ice cream and cake," she whispered.

Earl Brogdon stood in the back of the room. "I want to pray that my wife gets well."

"Is your wife sick, Mr. Brogdon?"

"Yes, ma'am." He glanced away, uncomfortable at the continued sound of his own voice. "My son told me so."

"We certainly will include her in our prayer. And our own Mrs. Fulbright, also. Is there anyone else who has someone or something special they would like to pray for?"

Emit Street cleared his throat. "If I don't get rid of this arthritis in my leg, I want to pray that God takes me."

Sister Clyeda's face colored. "Mr. Street"—she spoke to him curtly—"why don't we pray instead that He will give us the courage and strength to live the rest of our lives in His service." She gave him a long look. "Let us pray," she announced and folded her hands.

Sarah sat in his living room absently kicking the skirt of his couch, her legs covered in thick blue stockings. "And stop signs are red," she continued, "and flowers are. And cows are red."

"Cows are red?" Ira questioned. "Cows are not red, dear. They are brown."

She tossed her head, her black eyes brightening. "The one in our book is red!" she defied. "I showed it to you. Don't you remember?"

"Ah, so you did. Go on."

"I don't know any more."

He smiled at her pout. "You must know at least one more. What color was the ribbon you had in your hair yesterday?"

She giggled and pushed several fingers into her mouth coyly. "Red."

"You see, there *was* something else."

"And ketchup."

"Ketchup! Very good." He took a sip of his mint tea. "That was a wonderful one."

"And houses and flowers and cars."

"You said flowers."

"And flowers," she insisted. "And chimneys and wagons."

"Yes, that is all true. I used to have a red car, a long time ago."

"We used to have a car." Sarah came over to him, slapping her hand on his knee. "Did you know that? We had a big car."

"Was your car red?" he teased.

"No!" She rolled her eyes at his ignorance. "Blue."

"And where did you go in your car?"

"To the store," she replied. She considered it further. "To the store and to the moon!" Her sweatered arms danced above her head.

"Are there any stores on the moon?" Ira asked.

Sarah nodded.

"And what did you buy?"

"We went in a spaceship."

"Of course. And what did you buy?"

"Ice cream."

He made a big face of disappointment. "Ice cream! And you didn't bring me any."

"I ate it."

"You ate it." He shook his head sadly. "You must not love me very much."

"I do!" Sarah Aberdeen protested and clasped her arms about his neck. "It was melting."

"But I would have brought you something if I went to the moon."

"I did. It is at home. I will bring it tomorrow."

"Is there anything red on the moon?"

"Mr. Snow. Mr. Snow."

Ira blinked his eyes. The veiled circle was missing from the curtains. It must be late afternoon. He had thought it was much earlier.

"Mr. Snow." Bess Turner spoke quietly. "I am sorry to wake you, Mr. Snow, but it is time for your vitamin. Just take this—here is your water—and you can go back to sleep."

Ira accepted the thimble-sized paper cup. Warm, too, he thought. Unseasonably so.

CHAPTER 7

Jimi June Hasbrook was intently studying a few wadded Kleenexes she had found in a neighbor's trash basket and did not notice Andrew Carlyle until he had passed her room five times. "Hey!" she called loudly when she finally spotted him. "Carlyle, where are you going?"

He returned to her doorway. "I'm walking. It's pouring outside."

"You just walking around?" It seemed senseless to her.

"What would you have me do in the middle of a hurricane? Take a walk to town? Dance in the streets? Humph!" He raised his head indignantly. "The rain blew the chairs right off the porch."

She shrugged. "You can come in if you want."

"I don't care if the farms dry up and the farmers starve," he continued hotly. "It would be better than this weather."

"You can come in," she repeated.

He ventured a few steps. "There's nothing else to do."

Jimi June smiled and pulled a cardboard box from

under her bed. "You want some saltines?" she asked, proudly displaying the box. "I took them from dinner the other night." She unwrapped a napkin packet and helped herself. "They're still good."

"No, thank you."

She smiled wryly. "If I had known you were coming I would have made some coffee."

"You live here alone?"

"Nah." She gestured toward the far bed. "She's off somewheres. I haven't seen her since before lunch."

"Give me one of those crackers." Andrew changed his mind.

"I don't like her."

"You should move."

"She yells at me."

"You should move!" he insisted in a spray of cracker dust. He was irritated, nervous.

"She is going to leave." Jimi June caught a thread of the bedspread with the uneven corner of her middle nail. "I don't want anybody else to move in. I'm tired of living with people."

"They're all worthless."

"I've never had a room of my own," Jimi June continued.

Andrew rubbed the top of his denim pants. "Why didn't you just rent one?" he demanded. "Go off to the city and get yourself a room? It would have been good for you."

Jimi June stood up carefully and with a self-conscious sway in her hips walked to the double bureau she shared with Azzie. Her back was to Andrew. She played with the heavy curl over her left eyebrow. "They wouldn't let you go off like that. I always wanted a room of my own with a cat."

"Who wouldn't let you go off like that? Have you got anything else to eat?"

"No," she lied.

"Who are you talking about?"

"The doctors at the hospital where I lived. Do you like gray cats?" She turned around to face him.

"You lived in a hospital?" Andrew appraised her suspiciously. "What was the name of that hospital? What town was it in?"

"Valorda."

"Hospital, my eye! You mean that insane house!"

Jimi June ignored his response. "I used to live in Rose Hill," she told him. "Right outside, on a farm. That's a big town. You ever been there?"

"When did you move?" He stood very straight, away from the wall.

Jimi June thought about it. "Sixteen, I guess." She smiled in her slow way. "I was just a kid. Pretty, too."

"Sixteen!" Andrew shook his head vehemently. "God, you must be—" he began but thought better of it. "I had a cat once," he told her instead.

She was interested. "A gray one?" she asked, sitting on the bed while he remained standing.

"Black as spades. He was okay. Not mean like some of them. Independent son of a gun."

"Black cats carry bad luck."

"Not old Sammy. You think Sammy put me here?"

"You can sit down," she decided abruptly. "I want a gray one. Not white. There's something wrong with the eyes on white cats."

"They wouldn't let you have one here."

"You had a cat?" she teased in reply. "Your wife let you have one?"

"My wife never told me what to do," Andrew responded angrily. "I had Sammy for nine years, until somebody took him. Never understood that. Why somebody would want an old cat like that. Not as if he was a kitten."

"Did she like the cat?"

"Angie? I suppose so. She never seemed to mind it when old Sammy stayed in the house with us. She certainly never told me he couldn't."

"That was her name?" Jimi June demanded.

"No." Andrew rearranged himself in the narrow vinyl chair he had taken. "Her name was Angelica. I couldn't stand it, told her so the first time I met her. Pious, pompous name. I never called her anything but Angie."

"I didn't have a husband."

"You told me." He wiped his hands on his pants. "I guess you didn't have a good chance, being where you were."

"There wasn't anybody anyway," Jimi June answered nonchalantly. "Some of them were crazy and most of them were women. Is Angie living here with you?"

"No, I told you she died thirteen years ago. Let me see, when was it? In March, I believe."

Jimi June arranged her skirt into a full circle on the bed. Her thin knees showed, and the white skin above her knees. "We used to have dances," she said.

"Humph!" His eyes were on her legs. "I used to love to dance. I never was any good at it, but I sure made a fool of myself whenever I got the chance."

"I know how to fox trot."

Andrew stood up. "I better be going now. I was wondering." He gestured awkwardly. "Did they ever let you out?"

"Nah." She shook her head. "We had the dances right there. Do you know how to cha-cha-cha?"

"I better go," Andrew repeated. "I've got to stay loosened up."

"Loosened up?" Jimi June looked away, disappointed. "Okay. I've got things to do anyway."

He paused in her doorway. "I'll see you at dinner?" he asked.

Jimi June responded with the slightest smile. "I am always at dinner," she agreed.

Except for Andrew Carlyle, the rain put everyone in good humor, and permission was given for a bingo party on Saturday night. Dorothy Tyler and her friend, Fronie MacDermott, were unnaturally lucky at the game, and in the spirit of the cooler weather announced at dinner that they would give away some of their winnings—coupons redeemable for a free Coke or an extra dessert (when someone on a restricted diet bingoed, he was allowed to choose something of comparable value, such as a new pocket comb or a plastic pen). Henry Parker had no use for any of this, and he persuaded Ira to join Uncle Robert, Dr. Whitwell, and himself in a game of dominoes.

They were playing in the foyer of the lobby, where a card table had been set up. It was cooler there and, as Henry Parker pointed out, they could take full advantage of the breeze admitted by the opened front door. The moon was just rising as they began.

"I think there should be a time limit."

"Now, don't you look at me, Henry," Uncle Robert cried. "I don't take any longer than anybody else, and besides, you all know about the trouble I've been having with my new glasses. It's not fair if I put down a six-five thinking it's a double six just because you've rushed me."

"I'll give him a kick, Henry."

"See that you do, Doc."

Ira played games only to make a fourth when he was needed, as he was tonight, but he was a much better gamesman than his sparse record would warrant. He and Henry Parker quickly won the first few sets.

"We've got to get moving," Dr. Whitwell complained, shuffling the dominoes.

"I think the rain has turned our luck sour," Uncle Robert said, yawning.

Ira reached for the dominoes and saw his two middle fingers jump. He quickly withdrew his hand and locked his offending fingers between his legs.

"Your draw, Ira."

"Yes," he agreed, not moving. "How's your book coming along, Adam?"

Dr. Whitwell brightened. "Not too bad. It's a job, remembering all those backs. Hundreds of them. I don't know of another chiropractor in the country who's done it."

"Come on, Ira," Mr. Parker complained. "You're holding up the game. Make your draw."

Ira timidly extended his left hand. There was no tremor, and he quickly selected his blocks.

"It's my play first, I believe." Ira placed the four-six in the center of the table. "Adam," he asked casually, "did anybody ever come to see you with some kind of nervous twitch? A spasm, I suppose you might call it. I was reading about a case like that the other day. I thought it might be interesting to include in your book."

Mr. Parker looked concerned. "I thought you were all through with that, Ira. You've been so much better the past few weeks."

"So I am," Ira assured him hastily. "I was just curious because I had read this article. No other reason."

"No, I can't say they ever did." Dr. Whitwell played the spinner and considered Ira's question. "I had one man who had a pretty unsteady hand, but that was from lifting too many glasses of whiskey to his mouth." Adam Whitwell chuckled. "I remember my grandmother used to say that people got the jerks, as she called them, because they didn't get enough sugar. I don't know if there's any truth to that; my grandmother was a big candy fancier. But I'll tell you one thing. After forty years' experience as a doctor—over forty, to lay naked the truth—there's one thing I'm convinced of and that's the merit in a lot of these homemade theories." He patted his forearm. "Nothing works better on a burn than a little oatmeal mixed with milk and put on like a plaster. I'll bet you never heard of that. And I take vinegar and honey, a teaspoon of each every day, and I will until I die." He glanced down at the table. "Damn, Robert! Is that the best you have?"

"That's the game," Mr. Parker declared.

At the same time Andrew Carlyle and Jimi June were sitting together in the community room, stiffly holding hands, Emit Street made up his mind to talk to Janie

Lipscomb for the first time. He was seated in one of the blue-and-white vinyl-covered chairs in the dining area, four tables away from the bingo game. He was eating a package of M&M's brought to him by his brother on the occasion of his biyearly visit several days before. "Hello! Janie!"

Janie had been watching the bingo game and turned around sharply, grinning when her name was called. Her rabbit was bedded in a secret spot behind her curtain, and she hugged a rubber doll to her stomach.

"What have you got there? Is that your baby?" he teased.

"Boom!"

"Boom yourself. Is that her name? Is that your name? Boom! Boom!"

Janie opened her mouth wide and thrust her shoulders back, shaking her head furiously like a horse neighing.

Emit took a long moment to watch her full breasts move. "Did you ever have one of these?" He held up a red M&M. "See? Come here and I'll show you something."

Janie stroked her doll's coarse blond hair.

"Come on," he coaxed. "Your baby will want to see this."

Janie stopped close to his face and studied the candy. Her cheeks and neck were smooth and pale but opaque. Untouched, he thought. "There's a little white double *m* on the front," Emit told her. "If you can find it, the candy's yours."

Janie touched her doll's nose to the red candy and walked away.

"You found it! Here." He called her back and reached

for her hand. "You can have it."

Janie dropped it on the floor and did a small dance.

"No, you moron." He held out a yellow M&M and dramatically placed it in her mouth. "You eat it. It's candy. Now don't you waste this one."

She accepted it readily, delighted that the game was continuing, and after some deliberation ate it in the same way.

"That's the stuff. Lord, it's step by step with you, isn't it? Come a little closer and I'll give you another one."

She pointed to her mouth and stepped forward, but Emit caught sight of an evening aide who had joined the nearby bingo group. "No, you just take this one, on second thought." He placed it carefully in her palm. "I've got to go now. But you like these M&M's, don't you?"

Janie smiled, tracing the bowed lips of her baby doll.

"Don't you worry. Yes, indeed," Emit Street declared. "I'll see to it that your little girl gets some more candy."

Other than game-playing and romance, there were few activities in progress this Saturday night. Many of the more sedentary residents were sleeping. A few affluent private television owners were tuned to the "Hit Parade," and one radio played soft jazz. Marsh Colloway checked his speed to accompany Mr. Brogdon on a night stroll of the halls, and Miss Zeagler, disappointed that no one had spoken to her during the evening, kissed off her lipstick on the corner of a Kleenex.

Kathleen Storrs was in her room, sleeping lightly. A letter to her husband lay unfinished on the table beside her. In 7C, Azzie Bowdin was taking advantage of her roommate's absence. She had cleared out her drawers and divided their contents into neat piles on her bed. Azzie picked up several pairs of tan underwear and smelled out the dirty ones, haphazardly throwing them toward the trash basket. She had placed her pocketbook on the table, where she would not forget it, and began the last stage of her preparations, holding every object on the bed close to her eyes while inspecting it minutely with her hands. In this way she chose the clothes and souvenirs that she wished to keep and later packed them away in a worn carpet satchel.

CHAPTER 8

It is chilly and dew damp on early summer mornings in East Texas, and Azzie was dressed in only a sheer blouse and cotton skirt and a square wool hat that just covered her gray bun. She sat far down in the porch chair, her arms grasping either shoulder, and she was dreaming of the trip she had taken with Harry to Minnesota when the snow had been thigh deep. But an observer would not have known this, might not care, and when Henrietta Newman came to work at six-thirty and discovered Azzie, she was impressed instead with Azzie's raucous snoring. "Just like a man," Mrs. Newman said to herself. Even Azzie's first words upon being awakened were punctuated with stuttering snores.

"What?" she asked, shaking her head blindly. "Who are you? My, you're here early."

"It's nearly seven. What on earth are you doing out here?"

Azzie raised herself in the porch chair. "You know, I don't see well, and I'm sure that I know you. Isn't your name Storey or Starvey?"

"Newman," she replied. "Henrietta Newman."

"Oh, yes! Henrietta Newman. You do a fine job, Henrietta." Azzie coughed. "Cold as a witch's tit out here, isn't it?"

"What are you doing out here this time of morning?" Mrs. Newman again demanded. "And all dressed up."

Azzie rubbed her hands over her attire and grinned mischievously. "I'll bet you didn't even know I had a getup like this, did you? My husband brought this blouse to me from New York. It's silk, one hundred percent."

Mrs. Newman was chilly herself and answered shortly, "It's pretty, but it's a little fancy to be going to downtown India. Is that what you're planning?"

Azzie felt for Mrs. Newman's hand and closed her fingers around it tightly. "I'm waiting for Peggy. This is the day she is coming, you know. It's been such a long time since I have seen her; I don't remember when. Are you going to miss me?"

"Peggy? She is your daughter, isn't she? I haven't heard anything about your daughter coming today."

"Well, she is. I'm going back to Louisiana with her. Say, I wonder if she will bring the kids." Azzie brightened. "She couldn't bring them all, wouldn't fit in her car. One of those foreign cars, you know the kind I mean? Blue." She giggled. "Like riding in a snake's belly. That's how I'm going to Louisiana." She giggled again.

Mrs. Newman spoke softly. "How long have you been waiting out here?" she asked.

"Goodness, I don't know. Today is Sunday, I'm certain of that. I thought she might want to come early—

Peggy doesn't like to miss church—so I jumped out of bed this morning I don't know what time it was, but blind as I am, I swear it was before the sun. My things were already packed," she added with a note of pride.

"You must be tired of sitting out here. Why don't you come on back inside with me. It feels like it might rain again."

Azzie shook her head. "I'm not tired," she declared firmly. "I'm going to stay out here and wait for Peggy. She might not know where to find me if I didn't."

"You can sit in the front office," Mrs. Newman offered. "I'm sure Mrs. Johnston won't mind, and Peggy will spot you as soon as she comes in the door. Come on, dear." She raised Azzie's plump elbow. "Peggy will have to come inside anyway to get you all checked out."

"Oh, no." Azzie opened her pocketbook and triumphantly waved two cards and a bottle half filled with pink pills. "I am all ready to go." She peered in the direction of Cullum Street, her eyes focusing only as far as the edge of the porch. "I have all my things and I am leaving as soon as Peggy gets here."

"Have you got your records again? Give them to me, Azalea."

"No!"

"Give them to me so that I can put them back before Mrs. Johnston finds out and you get into trouble."

"These are my things." Azzie's back stiffened. "They have my name. You stole them from me and I am never going to give them back!"

Henrietta Newman reached for the cards. "Azalea."

"Leave them alone!" Azzie swung her purse broadside

into the woman's chest. "Filthy bitch! You want my money!" The purse caught Mrs. Newman's mouth. "You are trying to steal my money!"

"Excuse me." Dr. Howard Cannon addressed the woman sitting by the window. Her back was turned to him. "I am looking for someone, if you could help me." She did not answer and he took a hesitant step into the room. "Excuse me."

Kathleen turned her head. "Yes? I am sorry, I must not have heard you knock." She waved her hand. "I was daydreaming."

"I was looking for someone," he repeated, his hand nervously twisting the doorknob, "and I was told that she might be in this room." He glanced around quickly. "Does someone else live here?"

Kathleen followed his eyes to the single bed. "I am the only one," she answered pleasantly.

Kathy could not live in a place like this, Dr. Cannon thought to himself. The story must have been confused; perhaps Kathleen was ill and in a hospital nearby. But not in a place like this. "It's a mistake," he said out loud. "I apologize for disturbing you."

Kathleen was weary of her solitude. "Who was it you wished to see?"

"A Mrs. Storrs. Kathleen Storrs. You haven't heard of her, by any chance?"

"Well, the name rings a bell. Catchy name, don't you think?"

"Yes. What?" He was confused. "You have heard of her?" His eyes were caught by the thick yellow bun at her neck.

"I am Mrs. Storrs."

"I am sorry." He moved closer. "You have such a soft voice."

She spoke up. "I am Kathleen Storrs."

He chuckled awkwardly. "This is most confusing," he said, but at the same time studied her eyes and smile. "Are you from Cambria?"

"Yes, I am," she answered and leaned forward eagerly. "Tell me, do you know me?" Her small hand was suddenly clasped to her mouth. "Oh, no!"

"What is it?"

"Oh, no!" she breathed. "It's not—you're not Phillip, are you? I'm so terrible at faces now." She seemed to bite her hand. "No, of course not." Her voice began to lower. "No." She spoke to herself. "Phillip would tell me right away. He wouldn't— Who are you? Please."

"Howard Cannon." He reached her. "Are you all right? I am a doctor."

She was still distressed, and he stood close to her. Kathy's hair was a light auburn, he thought. This could not possibly be she. Yet Phillip had been her husband's name.

"I don't remember." She shook her head.

"I lived next door to you in Cambria. It has been a while." He paused. "You are from Cambria?" he asked again.

"Oh, yes." She began to recover. "Do you remember my house?" she asked. "White brick with a big wooden porch. I painted that porch myself one summer and put out wicker chairs. I hope the weather hasn't gotten to them."

"Yes, yes, I do remember. I sat in them many times."

He couldn't get over his bewilderment. "Kathy, I just can't believe it. I didn't realize it had been such a long time."

"Is that what you called me? Phillip always calls me Katy. Do you know my husband also?"

"Yes, certainly."

"Then I must write to him that I have seen you. What did you say your name was? I am sorry to be so forgetful."

"Dr. Howard Cannon. But what were you saying about Phillip?"

"He will be so sorry that he missed you. Phillip loves to see people. He is away on one of his trips, but he promised this will be the last." She laughed. "Don't let me go on. This is my favorite subject. Tell me all about what you have been doing so that I can write to him. Are you still living in Cambria?"

"I just moved back to a duplex the other side of town. I have been living in the East."

"Phillip has been thinking of getting one of those duplexes when we go back, but I want to keep our old house. Does your wife like it?"

He was startled. "I am not married."

"Oh." She nodded. "What part of the East?"

"Around Boston."

"That must be lovely. Phillip says so. He brought me an umbrella from Boston once."

Dr. Cannon took a seat in a wooden chair opposite her. "Where exactly is Phillip?" he asked cautiously.

"Exactly? He is on a trip. I am sure he gave me a list of cities where—" She paused. "Red lollipops! You used to give them to your patients."

"That's right." He nodded, pleased.

Kathleen was puzzled. "Now, why would I remember that and nothing else? Do you still?"

"I treat mostly adults now."

"I will have to write all of this to Phillip. I just hope I can remember."

"How long have you been living here?" he asked.

"Let me see." Kathleen turned her head to the window. "A day or two for certain. A week seems a little long. It's only a temporary arrangement, you understand. Just until Phillip comes for me." She smiled graciously. "We will have to see a great deal of each other in Cambria. Phillip will be so delighted."

Kathleen walked to her dresser, pulling her blue sweater closer around her thin shoulders. "I write to him every day," she said and shyly produced her gold box. "I expect a letter today with his new address." She carried the box to her visitor. "I have been saving all of these to send."

"Phillip . . ." Howard Cannon began. "Kathy, Phillip is . . ."

She was examining one of the blue packets. "I tie them up every week. But what were you saying?"

"Phillip will be glad to receive them, I am sure." He stood. "I must be going."

"Oh, no, not so soon," Kathleen protested, laying the box aside. "I haven't heard nearly enough about you. Phillip will be so interested."

"I am sorry. I must get back to my office. I still have patients today."

She extended her hand; her fingers were bony and cool. "Tell me, did we know each other for a long time?"

"Yes."

She pressed his hand. "Please come again."

"Certainly," he lied. "Is there anything you need, Kathleen? Money, books? Food?"

"No, no, I have everything. This is really quite a nice motel, and I brought writing paper."

"Well." He paused. "Kathy." He pulled her a step toward him in a quick embrace, one hand on her sharp backbone and the other resting on her circle of hair.

Azzie shook her head dreamily and raised her shoulders precariously off the pillow. Her weak vision rested first on a tray of cold lunch by her bed, and then on Jimi June, who was coming through the doorway. "Peggy!" she cried, elated, desperately squinting her parrot eyes. "I have been waiting for you. Look! The meal is all cold, but we can still eat." She wiped some moisture from her mouth. "I have told you to be on time to dinner, Peggy. I have been waiting quite a while."

"What?" Jimi June stopped. "What are you muttering about?"

Azzie's eyes were hurt by the light and she covered them. "Is that you, Peggy?"

"What are you talking about?"

Azzie shook her shoulders timidly and laughed. Her dark skirt had wrapped itself like a hot towel around her hips and she pulled at it weakly. "I must have been dreaming. Look at me!"

Jimi June did not move. "Who is Peggy?" she asked.

"I am so blind, Jimi. Thank God you are not blind like me."

"You scared me. Yelling at me like that with somebody else's name."

Azzie covered her bare ankles with a square comforter and fell back, closing her eyes on a dizzy head. "They must have given me some dope, Jimi. They want me to keep quiet. They gave me a shot of dope."

"Who is Peggy?" Jimi June persisted, lying similarly on her bed. "Do you know her?"

"My daughter."

"You must be crazy."

Azzie opened her eyes and struggled to focus. "You coon! Don't you talk to me about crazy." She caught her breath and began to recite carefully, "Peggy lives in Louisiana. She is coming to get me any day now. Perhaps today. This week. I am going back to Louisiana with her, have an operation on my eyes."

"Is that true?" Jimi June rolled over, one arm loosely wrapped about the pillow. A slight breeze from the open window nudged her with the idea of sleep. "Are you really going away?"

"Certainly. You don't think I am going to spend the rest of my days here."

"Do you think they will move anybody else in here when you are gone?"

"I don't know," Azzie replied, uninterested. "When I have the operation, I will be able to see. I am going to the Veterans Hospital." She raised her brow in a closed-eyed smile of confidence. "You see, Harry was a veteran. I am so blind now, that is why I couldn't see who you were."

"They better not get that Mrs. Zeagler in here." Jimi

June yawned. "I can't stand the way she prisses around."

"Don't worry." Azzie, too, was almost asleep. "They'd never find another soul saintly enough to put up with you." She snorted, "Saintly or stupid."

"I hope not. One stupid Mormon is enough."

CHAPTER 9

He could remember just how their afternoons together began. The day posed the threat of the first frost of the year and Ira had come home early from the newspaper office to cover his rosebush with burlap. Sarah spotted him and ran behind the sycamore that separated their yards. Her head was wrapped in a purple scarf so that only part of her nose and her two black eyes showed when she every now and again peeked out. The fringed tail of the scarf blew behind her.

Ira heard her giggle and looked up. "Cold," he muttered.

She laughed again.

He was shy and bent over his roses, securing the burlap with strings and heavy stones. "Is that you laughing, rosebush?" he asked after a moment.

"No. It's me."

"You!" He twisted his neck to address the sycamore. "I didn't know trees could talk. I never heard of such a thing."

Sarah hesitated.

"What a remarkable tree."

She ventured a step or two forward. "It's not a tree."

"Well, my goodness." He turned away from her and began picking up a pile of loose leaves. "How are you, Sarah?"

"Fine. How are you?" she returned politely.

"I'll tell you." Ira pulled up a dead weed. "I would be just great if I could solve one little problem."

"My mother has a problem," Sarah offered.

"Oh? What is that?"

"Me!" She giggled, delighted.

Ira smiled. "Well, you're not my problem, so maybe you could help me solve it. It seems that somebody gave me this whole package of peppermints and two bottles of pop. Now, I like both of those things, and I've been known to put away a considerable amount of them in my day. But I certainly couldn't eat all this much. I've looked everywhere for someone to help me. You wouldn't be interested, by any chance?"

Sarah thought it over. "I guess so. If you really need somebody."

After that day, Ira came home early more days than not, and sometimes Sarah would return to the newspaper office with him and make dolls and mobiles out of his old editorials while he finished the week's edition. In the spring they went off every day. Sarah's favorite walk was to the forest, as she called it, which Ira insisted was a euphemism for charred cans and maple sprouts. He would see things differently if they had horses, Sarah retorted. Since they did not, she perfected a neigh, which she would give with a great foot-shaking and nodding of her head as they turned past the Gulf station and onto a path forged by tire tracks.

There were times when they felt like a change and would go fishing off a bridge outside town, casting into a narrow green body called Dry Watson's Creek. Or on lazy days, and often in the summer, they just went to the pharmacy for a fountain Coke, or over to the schoolyard. Sarah would aim with furious determination for the bottom branch of a nearby elm, trying to raise some breeze with the tree and the swing and her skirt. Ira sat in the next swing, hardly moving, and burrowed his toes into the cool pebbles underneath until he noticed that it was ten of six or five of six. The great race home would then begin, both swearing they would never make it in time. Sarah's dinnertime.

"Good-bye, Mr. Snow."

"Good night, Sarah. Hurry inside now; your mother will be angry. But, Sarah"—his silky finger brushed hers —"we'll have to work on your swinging tomorrow. I believe that old tree is growing still."

"What is that!"

"Boom!"

"Oh, Robert—it's that Lipscomb woman."

"My God." Uncle Robert stared at the bleeding and bucktoothed monster face leering at him. "It's not time for Halloween yet, is it?"

"What are you doing out on this porch?" Dr. Whitwell demanded of her and leaned close to Uncle Robert. "Janet I think her name is. Go on inside, Janet," he ordered. "You're not supposed to be out here, certainly not like that. Go on."

Janie pushed her tongue through a slit in the monster mask.

"Don't do that at me," Uncle Robert cried with a shiver. "I swear to God, Adam, my sympathies are all with the unfortunate, but she gives me the creeps. Wait until I tell Cranson."

"Boom! Boom!" The sound was muffled and unsatisfactory and Janie retreated inside, feeding herself an M&M through the barred teeth.

"I think the sun is fixing to come out," Dr. Whitwell declared.

"Yes," Uncle Robert agreed, watching the door. "Is she gone for good?

"The rain has been good for the crops."

"I should say."

"I am afraid it will get hot again."

"What is this? Almost August. Halloween isn't for three months. I wonder where she got that mask."

"August will be hot," Dr. Whitwell persisted.

"It always is," Uncle Robert replied. "Wait until I tell Cranson about this. Course, he doesn't believe half the things I tell him about the people around here."

Dr. Whitwell resisted the obvious comment. "You feel like a round of gin this afternoon?"

"I could see it." Uncle Robert stretched his legs.

"Well, maybe I'd better not." The doctor reconsidered and rolled his chair to the edge of the porch. "Monica is supposed to come by and help me finish my chapter. That doesn't mean she will, of course." His voice began to sour. "She is so irresponsible nowdays. I don't know what gets into her. I wish she would get married. . . .

"Don't laugh," he admonished as Uncle Robert chuckled to himself. "I am not going to be around forever. Not that I do her a whole lot of good, crippled like I am."

"Children are going to do what they want, come what may," Uncle Robert declared axiomatically.

"Do you know what Monica is doing?" Dr. Whitwell responded angrily. "Writing ads for some jerk selling mobile homes." He ran his fingers along the wheels of his chair. "I should have sent her away from here when her mother died."

"She was only two!"

"I should have sent her away."

"Come on." Uncle Robert tried to reverse the direction of the conversation. "One round of gin. Just to five hundred. Cranson is sleeping this afternoon, and I feel like the company."

Dr. Whitwell studied the deserted Cullum Street. "All right," he agreed. "Monica will be late at any rate. If she comes at all."

August came to India, Texas, as breezy as a week in spring, but Azzie was ruled by the thick sleep of phenobarbital those first cool days. By the second Tuesday, when the dosage was at last modified, the air was still and hung like warm syrup around her bed. Azzie lay tired from the night until eleven-thirty, when a woman came in with her luncheon tray.

"Look at me!" Azzie laughed uncertainly and pulled at a mat of hair over her ear. "I'm all in pieces."

"Look at you!" It was Henrietta Newman. She pointed

irately to the last of a bluish bruise on her face. "Just look at me," she returned. "This is what you did."

"My, my, my." Azzie shook her head. "You know, I'm so blind I can't see it, but I am sure it is just terrible. What did you bring me for lunch?"

"I can see you are feeling fine."

"Actually"—Azzie rolled onto her side and raised her nightgown—"I feel a little something right here." Her hands explored two raw bedsores on her hip.

"You need a bath, all right," Mrs. Newman answered. "I believe tomorrow is your day, and I'll see if Grace can wash that hair and put it in some sort of order. You aren't scheduled for the beauty shop, but maybe Vidy would switch."

"Oh, and honey"—Azzie lifted one short leg—"I need another pair of hose. I had to throw most of them out. They were so bad."

"I'll see what I can do," Mrs. Newman replied. "We're short on hose."

Azzie weakly wiped her face and arms with a towel. The trick, she thought, was to keep yourself dry. That was how Harry had made it through the World War without even a bath, simply depending on towels or rags and leaves in bad times. Thinking of Harry, she put on a pair of quartz crystal earrings he had brought her from the Grand Canyon and tied a green scarf around her disheveled hair. She wanted to look at least sane for her first encounter with the front office in weeks.

"Hello!" Azzie called out cheerfully and gave a tap with her cane. "Is anybody in there?"

The sounds of a typewriter stopped. "Come in," Ima Johnston replied in her tart voice. "Yes, come in."

Azzie pushed on the door. "Well, I can't see." Her hands found the knob and the door opened quickly. "Here I am." She giggled. "And all out of breath. You know I haven't seen daylight since—" She jerked her head up. "What day is it anyway? You know I walked all the way up here from my room."

"That's quite a ways," Ima Johnston agreed. "And I ought to know: I built the place." She gave a hearty laugh. "I did indeed."

Azzie smiled patiently.

"I'm sort of busy today, Azalea." She indicated the clutter of her desk. "Why don't you go out to the porch and rest awhile? I'm sure the men would love to have a lady join them. If you behave yourself." She waved a large finger. "I'll have no hanky-panky in my house."

"Hanky-panky," Azzie repeated and dismissed it. "You know, I was wondering if I had any mail."

"If there was anything for you, you would have gotten it on your tray this morning." She raised her hands above her gray Smith-Corona. "Now I've got to get back to work."

Azzie clucked her tongue. "You work too hard. You ought to get yourself a secretary." She smiled affably. "I was thinking that I might hear from Peggy."

"You just got a letter from Peggy," Mrs. Johnston replied. "You can't expect to hear so often. You will be disappointed."

"I haven't heard from Peggy in some time," Azzie corrected her. "I wish that I would. She is coming for me. I am going back to Louisiana for an operation."

"Azalea Bowdin," Mrs. Johnston demanded incredulously. "Don't you remember the letter I brought you just last week from Peggy? The one with the pictures in it?"

"I haven't gotten a letter from anybody."

Ima Johnston searched through her top drawer. "I think I might still have it. I don't usually save letters after they have been read, but this one had her new address on it—she's living in Oklahoma now—and I haven't had time to change it in your records. Oh, here it is." She produced a daisied envelope. "I declare, you have the memory of a two-timer. Do you want me to read it to you again?"

Azzie seated herself clumsily in a vacant chair. She said nothing but leaned forward so intently that her knees brushed Mrs. Johnston, who began:

" 'Dear Mother, I have been informed in a letter from one of the aides at your home that you are depressed and want me to come and see you. You mustn't let your spirits get down, Mother. Count all the blessings the Lord has given to you, all of the wonderful years you had with Daddy, and the life you still enjoy. Remember what Daddy always said—being happy is ninety-nine percent just making up your mind to it.

" 'I cannot come to see you now. It is impossible with summer school and getting moved into our new home. If I don't have to teach again next summer, perhaps I will come then.

" 'All the children are fine and say hello to Grandma. Don't make trouble, Mother. Mrs. Johnston has been so good to you.

" 'You are in my prayers. Peggy.' "

"Do you want to see the pictures?" Ima Johnston asked and held up two black-and-white snapshots of the kind taken in grammar school. "These must be your grandchildren. What are their names, Azalea?"

Azzie stared at the blurred faces. "I don't remember."

"The little girl has a nice face. I hope she keeps that blond hair. They don't look nearly so cute if it turns dark." She examined a much larger photograph. "This must be Peggy."

Azzie accepted the picture and studied it closely. "She's old. The woman in the picture is old."

"I know what you mean. It's hard to believe that your children get old, too." She guffawed. "I can't believe it about myself, to tell you the truth. You go along now, Azalea. I have a nursing home to run. Oh, no," she protested as Azzie laid the photograph on her desk. "It's for you. You keep the others, also."

Azzie staggered to her feet. "I have a mirror," she declared. "If I want to look at an old woman, that's all I have to do."

"Come on in and take off that face," Emit Street commanded.

Janie did not move.

"Come on! You've been wearing that mask for days. Oh, hell." He reached under his mattress and tore open a bag of gumdrops. "You've already gone through the M&M's and the Milk Duds," he told her irately. "Here you go."

Janie came for the candy eagerly and he quickly raised it above his head. "Take your mask off," he ordered.

She grabbed for his hand.

"No! No!" He pushed her skirt between her thighs and moved closer. "I ain't putting my hands on no monster."

Janie was angry and she wiggled free.

"Come back." Emit Street caught her shoulder. "All right." He turned her toward him and pushed the candy into her mouth, his right hand coming up to cup her breast. He leaned his head on the monster's shoulder while Janie chewed.

It was after two when Jimi June returned from her soap opera. Azzie was sitting in the room's only chair, holding her writing pad in her lap. "I've been waiting for you." She smiled.

"Waiting for me?" Jimi June was suspicious. "What do you mean, waiting for me?"

"I need your help. I need the help of your two good eyes. I could do it myself, but the good Lord has seen fit to reclaim my sight." She looked down at her lap pitifully.

"Well, I don't want to help you." Jimi June lay on her bed, her face flattened against the sheet. "They washed these sheets," she announced. "They smell so good."

Azzie jumped abruptly in her chair. "They won't let me out of here, Jimi!"

Jimi June was not interested. "What do you mean? Peggy is coming to get you."

"I don't know anyone named Peggy."

"What?" She sat up angrily. "You said your daughter Peggy was coming to get you. You swore she was. Any day, you said."

"She's dead."

Azzie's roommate took a long moment to judge her earnest figure. Azzie tried to level her eyes and gripped the arm of the chair to testify to her sincerity. "She's dead."

"How did she die?" Jimi June questioned cautiously.

"She fell down. I need your help, Jimi. You've got to help me."

"I don't want to."

"I'll pay you."

Jimi June paced about the room.

"I'll pay you," Azzie pressed.

"You don't have all of your mind," Jimi June told her from the window.

"I have a lot of money," Azzie retorted with importance. "Harry was very rich and when he died every penny of it went to me."

"Who was Harry?"

"My husband, Harry. I will put you in my will."

"Where is he?"

"Dead. I told you that; you never listen." Azzie raised her brow. "If Harry were still alive, I never would have seen this place."

"I'm tired," Jimi June said and stretched out on her bed once again. "Shut up and let me go to sleep."

"Jimi." She leaned forward and spoke with great intensity and patience. "I want you to write a letter for me. That is all. I will put you in my will for fifty dollars."

"You'd better shut up now."

"I'm going to leave you a hundred dollars for writing me this short note."

Jimi June raised up on an elbow. "What would I do with a hundred dollars? I have no place to spend it."

"You could leave it to this place," Azzie continued

with uncharacteristic civility. "They would build a room in your honor. With your name on it."

"Really?" She thought it over. "I don't think they would do that. They have a lot of rooms."

"Yes, they would. Or maybe a little terrace with chairs around so people could sit outside in the backyard and get away from those old fools on the front porch. And right in the middle would be a brick that said, 'Donated by Miss Jimi June Hasbrook' and the date of your death." Azzie pictured it with her hands. "I would make sure they did that."

"Who is the letter to?"

Azzie grinned broadly, anticipating her triumph. "To the Shriners. Harry was a Shriner, one of the founding fathers of the Hella Temple in Mantis. That's where we lived when we were not traveling. I want to write to them."

"All right."

She thrust the pad and pencil at Jimi June. "Now," she directed, "put the date across the top so that it looks official. Today is the ninth."

Jimi June returned the pad. "You write first that you are going to leave me a hundred dollars. I am not writing any letter until you do."

"I'm so blind."

"I'll write it." Jimi June reclaimed the paper and wrote in a painstaking hand: "I, A. Bowdin, will pay Miss Jimi June Hasbrook one hundred dollars. This is August 9, 1956."

"Don't you think my name is nice?" Jimi June remarked.

"Write my letter now."

"You have to sign this first."

"I can't see."

"You can put an X on it."

Azzie furiously clutched the pencil given her and traced an oversized "A.B." "All right. Now in God's name write my letter!"

Jimi June was compliant. "Who is this to again?" she asked.

Azzie pondered. "Make it to the President," she decided. "The President of the Hella Temple in Mantis."

"Hell's temple?"

"Hella, you idiot! H-e-l-l-a, Hella. Did you put the date?"

"Yeah."

"Dear President of the Hella Temple," she dictated. "My friend,"—she made a sour face—" is writing this for me because I am blind."

"Slow down," Jimi June cried.

"I am blind and I fall into things and I can't see to eat my food. I am eighty-four years old and I shall be dead in a few weeks of starvation."

"I am only sixty-six." Jimi June smiled.

"My husband, Harry S. Bowdin, was one of your founding fathers. In fact, I believe that I am the only living widow of one of the founding fathers of the Hella Temple."

"Founding fathers?" Jimi June stopped. "What does that mean?" She grinned mischievously. "What do they find?"

"They found the scissors I am going to use to cut up this piece of paper if you don't shut your stupid mouth." Azzie waved the initialed statement. "You hear me?" She continued calmly. "Please help me if you want me to stay alive, for I am very much convinced that I cannot hold out here much longer.

"I am in India, Texas, in the Twilight Days Rest Home." She paused. "Jimi, do you know the street address here?"

"No."

"I guess he can find it."

"He can have his father find it."

"Give it to me and let me sign it," Azzie directed. "No, first put 'Sincerely' down at the bottom—No, I know: 'Praying for your swift arrival.' Now let me sign it."

"I thought you were blind," Jimi June scoffed.

"Give it here."

Jimi June held out an empty hand. "I want my paper to the hundred dollars."

Azzie fed the slip to her grasp and received the letter in return. "Mrs. Harry S. Bowdin," she slowly produced and in an illegible hand repeated her plea: "Please help me."

CHAPTER 10

Dorothy Tyler closed her eyes tightly and flipped her dictionary open to a random page. Her long-nailed middle finger ran down the left side of the paper, then stopped; she opened her eyes. "Risibility," she read. "Laughter. Merriment. The ability to laugh." "I am risible," Dorothy Tyler repeated to herself. "Rise" was right around there and "risk," "risking," "roach," "roadhog," "roadster."

"Orgh mam wurst laba in tran ox, laba in tan bog ox, ona isa purdy!" Elberta Peterson smiled at the white rag rope binding her in a wheelchair. "Hony herme ad ise dien non, non. Duhute mamos leder."

Dorothy Tyler tried again. Page 457. "Jingo . . . One who favors a—"

"Duwa ige iaise on ch ia neveth ooses whj on awk a on ie."

Mrs. Tyler slammed her book closed. At eighty-seven, Dorothy Tyler had no regard left for men at all and little for women except as card partners. When not involved in a game of casino or go fish, they could be extremely tiresome and dull, especially when they were sick or into a fit, a condition her roommate seemed to be enjoying at the moment.

"Shut up!" Dorothy Tyler commanded.

Elberta Peterson kicked at her chair and giggled. "Exech aniemail andy pirch en or e iond! Weec rair porry."

Mrs. Tyler clasped her hands resolutely and bowed her head. " 'Four score and seven years ago,' " she began.

"Come on, dear, step out of your dress," Bess Turner instructed Azzie, who stood with her moist uncovered toes curled toward the floor.

"Where are you?" Azzie asked anxiously. "I have to hold on to you."

"I am right here. Now give me your hand and pick up your feet. That's right. No, now you're stepping on your hem. Pick up your feet, Azalea."

Jimi June was already naked. She sat on the floor watching the water fill the twin bathtubs. Just like our beds, she thought, and yawned. Her hands slid along the pink tiles. They were warm from the wall furnace and smooth to sit on.

"I am going to put some vaseline on those sores when you get out," Mrs. Turner declared, placing her hand on a raw patch of Azzie's hip. "I don't know why these things refuse to heal, but until they do, I am going to rub a tablespoon of vaseline on them every week."

"Well." Azzie stared blindly around her. "I hope it helps."

"Come on, Jimi."

Jimi June obediently rose to her feet. Her attention

was captured by the vision of naked familiarity presented to her by a mirror hanging the length of the bathroom wall.

"Is that too hot?" Bess Turner asked, dipping Azzie's foot in the water.

"No." She laughed, gripping the edge of the tub. "It's just fine as long as I don't fall in; you hold on to me."

"You're not going to fall. I've got you. Jimi, I told you to come on."

"Is your name Storey?" Azzie asked.

Jimi June rotated slowly. Her hips were fine, small. A loose but not plump stomach, she decided, circumscribing the front of her belly with her spread hands. Her nipples were red and plump. The color on her thighs was an uneven white but still the skin was soft to touch, covered with long light hairs. She followed the path down her knees and below, where the hair grew more thickly and dark. She touched her face, her hair.

"What are you doing? Your water is going to get cold if you keep playing like that, and I am not going to run it again."

Jimi June glanced back at the mirror. She wondered if Andrew had guessed at her body.

"Hurry up."

Without answering, Jimi June stepped into her bath. The water covered her, smoothing and reddening her skin, making her like the tiles.

She brought the face of the clock close to her eyes. It was eleven-thirty. Lying on her back in the dark, she had known before looking that it was late. Azzie had rolled about, issuing complaints and curses of discomfort, for hours before she finally got to sleep and now the honking sounds of her victory filled the room. Jimi June put on some paper slippers and groped around in the dark for a blouse to button over her muslin gown.

The sudden glare of the hall light hurt her eyes, and Jimi June pressed her face against the door, taking a long moment to let the brightness seep between her eyelashes and lids. When she could focus on the wormish patterns in the floor, she cast a squinting glance down to the end of the ward. The desk was deserted, evidence that Frances Crawford, evening aide, was taking a nap on the cot she had provided for herself in the back of the laundry room. Jimi June yawned and stretched, her short arms reaching up in a loose arc above her head. She felt like exploring.

She began at the back door. Nothing could be seen from the window, but her palm on the glass told her that it was cooler outside than at any time during the day. Jimi June noted the fact and hurried on. Open doors enticed her with the different sounds of breathing. There was a cough somewhere and a sound of someone turning in bed. Jimi June became bold with her curiosity and ventured into doorways, bending closer and staying longer, daring to touch the bed sheets that covered lumpy shadows until one cried out at her. The harshness of the reproach coming from a sleeping world startled her and soured the game.

The beauty parlor was the first door off the lobby. It was not locked and Jimi June found the chain for the light after a little searching. The room had been a utility closet in the original farmhouse, and it was crowded with three chairs and a sink. The walls, except for two round mirrors, were decorated with pictures from movie magazines. Elizabeth Taylor and Marilyn Monroe vied for the most popular.

A large brown carton was pushed under one of the chairs and Jimi June pulled it out, seating herself on the floor next to it. It was filled with curlers and boxes. She selected several of these and set them in her lap, examining them one by one, giving thought to words like "hexachlorophene" and "bleach" and considerably more attention to the pictures decorating the front. At length she opted for a blond woman lying on her stomach in the grass, a blade between her lips. It was called Simply Beautiful.

Jimi June picked up a fat comb that had been left in the sink and pulled it through her coarse waves. She was impatient and quickly decided to open her selected package. Inside was a pamphlet filled with diagrams and pictures of the same blond woman and a clear plastic bag containing a red syrupy substance. She hesitated. It was not the yellow shade she had chosen, and she concluded that the package was old and had gone bad; she searched through the remaining boxes until she found another Simply Beautiful. To her consternation, the dye inside was the same scarlet hue.

It was cold to her scalp and she shivered, wrapping a towel around her neck to catch the trickle. She might as well use both packages, she thought, as long as she had them, and she fashioned a tall cone of bubbly curls.

It was after one. Jimi June wondered how long it would take the dye to turn blond; possibly a day or two. The excitement of her adventure had passed and a nap seemed in order. She moved one of the three chairs closer to the sink and, resting her brilliant head on the cool porcelain, she slept.

"You didn't eat your breakfast, Mr. Brogdon."

Earl Brogdon rolled over. "My ear hurts," he answered apologetically.

"He's a crybaby!" Max Churcher called out from the other bed.

"Is the pain very bad?" Mrs. Newman asked, collecting the untouched tray.

"I have to sleep on the other side every night. It feels —" He hesitated, glancing at Mr. Churcher. "Hurts," he summarized quietly.

"I will tell the doctor to look at it on Tuesday."

"Don't tell my wife," Earl pleaded, his voice rising. "If my wife comes, don't tell her. She worries," he explained. "Luisa worries about me terribly."

Max Churcher chuckled to himself.

Margot Zeagler crossed her legs, tediously smoothing a wrinkle in her skirt. She said nothing. Her eyes darted nervously in front of her.

Azzie encompassed Miss Zeagler's long profile in her smile. "How have you been, Miss Zeagler?" she asked.

"Fine." Miss Zeagler gave the wall a quick nod in response.

"Well! I'm glad to hear it! I didn't know how you were because I have been ill recently and not able to get around. But I am not surprised to hear that you are well. You are still young to me—an old, ancient"—she waved her arms wildly—"geezer like me!"

Miss Zeagler wet her finger and drew it across her lips. "I am seventy-two," she replied in a hushed voice.

"You don't mean it! You certainly don't look your age. You look a decade younger than that moron Jimi June I live with, and she's only sixty-six. I guess crazy people don't age as fast as the rest of us. You know she is crazy."

This brought a stolen look. "Really?"

"You didn't know that? She's been in the state loony bin almost all of her life, just like Vidy."

Miss Zeagler's timidity loosened with her fascination. "Did she kill someone?"

Azzie shook her head. "I don't know. No one will say. But it must have been something terrible, something as bad as murder, for them to lock her up like that for the rest of her life. She was only sixteen or twenty." Azzie folded her hands. "You can imagine what it is like to live with her. She is still a raving maniac after all that time. Bald now, too. She lost all her hair."

"I would be afraid."

"I am afraid!" Azzie stressed with a shudder. "And the terrible thing is that I am almost completely blind in this eye"—she winked—"and the other is almost as bad, so that I couldn't even tell if she were about to kill me. Someday you are going to hear that I have been found in some awful state and you will know that I was helpless to prevent it."

"Perhaps you would be safer in another room," Miss Zeagler offered.

"I have been in just about every one they have at one time or another, except with the men. I am going to get out of here. I am eighty-four years old, Miss Zeagler, and nobody is going to keep me here the last days of my life, and I don't kid myself about that. But I have to have help to get out."

"Don't you have any friends?" Miss Zeagler asked shyly.

"Thank God for my friends," Azzie answered. "I have a few and I treasure them, I want you to know that. My friends mean more to me than anything I own, although I own a lot of wonderful things." Azzie faced her companion, who recoiled under the scrutiny. "I count you as my friend, Margot."

"You do?" she whispered, turning her gaze to the floor.

"I think you are the only friend I have here, the only one who hasn't tried to use me or hurt me. They all want my money here," she continued to Miss Zeagler's shoulder. "They all want my money and that is why they don't want me to leave. But you are not that way, I know you're not."

"No!"

"That is why you are the only one I would feel right about leaving it to. My daughter has deserted me."

Miss Zeagler bowed her head.

"She has fixed it so that this place gets all my money while I am alive and she gets the rest when I go, not soon enough for her. Like a buzzard." She shook her head violently and her whitish eyes glistened. "No one I care about will get a cent. That's how it is to be old."

Miss Zeagler leaned toward Azzie. "I could never take your money."

"There won't be any!" Azzie cried. "They have stolen it, taken away the last rights of an old woman. If I could get out of here, I could get it back, I could change things. I have a friend, a very important friend," she emphasized. "He could spring me from this place. He could get me out of Sing Sing if he only knew where I was, but I am a prisoner here. I am too blind to write to him."

"I could write to him for you," Miss Zeagler offered, her voice so full of shyness it was almost inaudible.

"Can you write?" Azzie gave a great exclamation of amazement.

"Yes," Miss Zeagler answered, color filtering into her face with her eagerness and pride. "I can write to him for you."

Azzie pulled her wrinkled writing pad from her purse. "You have saved my life! Here is a pen. His name is Roscoe. Mr. Roscoe, R-o-s-c-o-e. He was my husband's boss. My husband, you know, was a buyer for Salinger's in C. City. Mr. Roscoe"—she paused—"is the president of Salinger's. And he told me once, at a lovely party he gave at his home, that Harry was one of the pillars of his organization. And he was. Harry was the best buyer they will ever see."

"What did he buy?" Miss Zeagler asked.

"Oh, everything!" She laughed. "Harry would buy anything and everything. But he had a great eye. Not junk, you understand. Fur coats. I had a fur coat. Now, have you got the date? I believe it is the fifteenth. I asked Mrs. Johnston this morning."

Miss Zeagler transcribed the date in a fine, tight hand. "Do you want me to put the time?"

"Just that it's afternoon. . . . Dear Mr. Roscoe," Azzie dictated. "I am the wife of your late buyer, Harry S. Bowdin."

"Harry with two *r*'s?" Miss Zeagler asked.

"Yes, dear. That is the only way it is ever spelled, I am quite sure.

"As you know," she continued, "Harry passed on five years ago last April. Since that time I have been at the mercy of the world. I have been robbed and left to die by my own daughter, who has put me away in a nursing home in India. They will not let me out, but even though I am eighty-four, I would walk out on my two good legs if I were not blind. I am thankful to God that he took Harry before he could live to see this.

"There is no food here that a person can eat," she went on, "and I shall die as my daughter wishes if someone doesn't help me. You are the only one I have to write, the only friend I have left in this world, except for Miss Margot Zeagler, who is writing this letter for me because I am blind. Miss Zeagler cannot help me to get out because she is kept here also.

"I pray to God that you will come.

"I am in the Twilight Days Nursing Home in India, Texas. I do not know the street address.

"Sincerely," Azzie concluded. "Have you got all that down?"

"Yes." Miss Zeagler nodded, impressed with Azzie's command of words. "Yes, I do. It is a wonderful letter."

"I want to wait to sign it until I have more light," she decided, inspecting the lines of handwriting with a close-up eye. "I think it looks all right. I will send it right after breakfast tomorrow." Azzie raised Miss Zeagler's light hand to her cheek. "You will be remembered for this."

Miss Zeagler whispered the words, trying to smother her one apprehensive thought in this moment of intimacy: "Will they let it out?" she wondered. "All the mail goes to Mrs. Johnston." She paused. "They want your money," she reminded.

"As long as I have a stamp!" Azzie declared triumphantly. "No one can stop the mails."

CHAPTER 11

This morning Kathleen Storrs was taking her first walk around Twilight Days. She had used the last of her blue stationery in a letter to Phillip last night, and there seemed to be nothing to do but to ask for some at the desk—motels usually had stationery they would give away or sell for a small price. Kathleen had dressed herself with a bit more care than usual this morning, choosing a brown plaid skirt and an old, pleated crepe blouse. She paused for a moment in front of her bureau mirror and brushed a few hairs away from her forehead. There seemed to be a certain thinness in her face she had not noticed before. Phillip had always said that she was prettiest when her face was a bit full, and Kathleen resolved to eat more of the potatoes and bread from her meal trays.

Mrs. Turner had given her directions to the front desk. She was to walk toward the bathroom, a familiar route, turn with the building, and keep straight until she came to the lobby. Kathleen was about to make that turn when she recognized Elberta Peterson sitting strapped in her wheelchair. Mrs. Peterson was talking furiously and waving her hands at the wall ahead of her. It was because Kathleen had paused to listen that she did not notice Azzie when she came around the corner.

"Well, hello!"

"Hello," Kathleen returned hesitantly.

"How are you?" Azzie inquired agreeably. "What is your name again?"

"Kathleen Storrs."

"Storrs! Why, I have been looking for you! Kathy Storrs. You're the one from Cambria. I thought you were going home."

"Yes, I am."

"You told me that two months ago."

"Two months?" Kathleen shook her head. "I have only been here a few days." She took hold of the railing that ran at waist level along the wall.

"I know perfectly well how long you've been here," Azzie corrected her. "It was the first of July and we are well into August. Say, I was wondering if you had heard from our friend Mr. Roscoe. That's what I wanted to see you about."

"I don't know a Mr. Roscoe."

"Well, he lives right there in Cambria. I just wrote him the other day. You know"—Azzie stepped very close to Kathleen, her breath on the taller woman's neck— "you're too thin. Peggy was once like you. She's not now —God, she's too fat—but when she was a little girl she would never eat. It worried me."

"They bring my meals to my room," Kathleen answered. "Everyone is so nice to me, but I don't seem to have much of an appetite."

Azzie listened to her and smiled broadly. "Yes!" she declared. "I know the problem."

"Well." Kathleen looked toward the turn in the hallway. "I was on my way to get some stationery."

Azzie only grinned.

"Thank you very much," Kathleen said again, still standing in her doorway. "That was very thoughtful of you."

Azzie dismissed it easily. "It was nothing. Jason Hadley goes to town all the time and he'll bring me anything. That old monkey." She giggled. "He'd bring me a whole grocery store if I crooked my finger."

"It looks delicious." Kathleen turned the apple over in her hand. "I don't know when I've had a piece of fresh fruit."

"I smelled it," Azzie told her pointedly. "And it smelled good. I thought I would take just a little taste."

"Oh, of course, I should have offered." Kathleen stepped back into her room. "Come in. Though I don't know what I have to cut it with."

Azzie settled herself on the bed, which was nearer than the chair and also larger, easier to see. With some delight she produced a pair of nail scissors from her purse. "I hope you don't mind. I haven't cut my nails with them in a long time. I'm afraid I'd take a finger off by mistake."

"I don't suppose I have anything else," Kathleen admitted, taking them from her.

"I think he's got things on his mind."

"Who is that?" Kathleen asked, handing her half of the apple.

"Jason Hadley. . . . My, that's good!" Azzie exclaimed

after taking a sizable bite. "Here, dear, you take the rest. I just wanted a nibble. I don't think I'll live to see the day when somebody says I'm getting too thin." She spoke thoughtfully. "I am eighty-four years old."

"You certainly get along well for your age."

"I am blind," Azzie answered sharply. "I fall into things all the time. I drank my specimen the other day. I thought it was some sort of juice, weak tea, but that doesn't mean I'm crazy. I just can't see. I've still got all of my mind, and believe me, Kathy, I'm going to get out of here." She shook her head and spoke in a lighter tone. "Imagine me wanting to bump around with a man now. Bless Jesus."

"What?" Kathleen questioned, biting into her apple.

"I loved Harry, mind you. I was crazy about him, but I never could get too excited about what he wanted to do. I always suspected there was something about all that business that Harry just didn't know. But if Jason Hadley ever knew, he's forgotten by now."

"Surely this Mr. Hadley . . ."

"Was it good?" Azzie asked. "The apple, I mean. I thought it was good, the little taste I had. Course, my teeth aren't what they used to be."

"Yes, it is very good. Thank you again."

"It was nothing. I'll get you another one sometime. But not too soon. I don't want to ask Jason for too many favors. Give him ideas."

"Have you known Mr. Hadley very long?"

"He was a friend of Harry's in the war. Same regiment over in France. Harry's passed on, you know. Five years ago."

"I'm sorry."

"So was I," Azzie declared after a long moment of consideration. "He was a good husband, a successful husband. Rich," she clarified further. "What does your husband do?"

Kathleen answered the question slowly. "He was a professor for years. A professor of history. Now he travels, but this is his last trip. An old neighbor of ours from Cambria was here just a few days ago. He told me Phillip would be coming for me anytime now."

"His name wasn't Roscoe, was it?"

"No. No, I don't recall his name; isn't that funny?" Kathleen laughed shortly and put her hand to her cheek. "I've known him for years. But I am sure it wasn't Roscoe."

"Mr. Roscoe is coming for me," Azzie told her, "just like your husband."

"I thought your daughter was coming."

"Not my daughter!" Azzie retorted harshly. "Mr. Roscoe, who was also a friend of Harry's, just like Mr. Hadley. He was his boss in C. City, where we used to live for years, but he was also Harry's personal friend. Mr. Roscoe is going to take me to the hospital." Azzie's voice rose. "He is a very powerful man, and when he comes nobody will be able to keep me here. I am not going to stay here, Kathy." She struck the bed with her palm. "I have made up my mind that they can't stop me."

"I am sure . . ." Kathleen began softly.

"I used to have beautiful eyes, Kathy. I'll bet you have beautiful eyes, if only I could see them. What color are your eyes?"

"Green."

"Mine were brown. I don't know what they are now."

Azzie shook her head. "They must be awful."

"Oh, no," Kathleen protested untruthfully. "Not at all."

"I'm sorry you have to see them." Azzie covered her face. "I'm going to stay in my room from now on so that nobody will have to look at such a sight. I was planning to go to the party tonight, but I will stay in my room with that bald Jimi June. They won't let her go anywhere."

"You should go," Kathleen urged her. She was distressed by Azzie's sudden mood. "You should get out and be with people. Just think about what a nice visit we are having right now."

Azzie smiled half-heartedly. "You are good to try to cheer up this old corpse, Kathy. But I don't want to go alone. If I had someone to go with, someone to talk to, maybe I wouldn't think about how I look. But nobody would want to go with me."

"What sort of party is this?" Kathleen inquired hesitantly.

"A *party* party. You know. Just the sort of thing I love." She directed her large clouded eyes toward Kathleen. "But there is no one who would go with me. Unless perhaps you . . . But don't say yes on my account."

"No." Kathleen made up her mind quickly. "I would be happy to go with you. I just have to write to Phillip and tell him where I will be."

"Good!" Azzie was delighted. "I will stop by for you at eight o'clock sharp."

"When is eight?" Kathleen wondered aloud. "I never know what time it is since I misplaced my watch. Heaven knows where."

"I can fix that." Azzie removed a gold watch from her

wrist. "Here." She dangled it in front of her. "Take this."

"Oh." Kathleen was embarrassed. "I didn't mean that. No, it's out of the question."

"Go on. I can't see the numbers anymore; it doesn't do anything but get in my way. Take it." She held it out further. "It's a good one. Harry got it for me. I want you to have it."

Kathleen was staring at the watch. Nine minutes after two. Lunch must come around eleven-thirty. She would check tomorrow.

Azzie was standing. "Be ready at eight. Oh, and Kathy, I can't see you very well but you look awfully dark from here. Wear a little color tonight. Men like color." Azzie smiled mischievously. "Just because we don't want to bump around with them doesn't mean we can't flirt a little."

Ira Snow and Henry Parker shuffled about their room, bickering about the coming election, which Mr. Parker said proved that the Democrats were working hand in hand with the Communists. Ira usually maintained a diligent silence during his friend's periodic railings, but this evening he was involved in getting dressed for the church party, and he absently fell into discussion.

"Which tie do you like, Ira?" Mr. Parker held up two narrow striped ties, one of which was silver with ribbons of green.

"The silver." Ira pointed. "What I can't understand, Henry, is why you think the Democrats would want to work with the Communists. They're not going to get money from—"

"Because they're Communists themselves!" Mr. Parker thundered. "Emit convinced me of that. The Communists are in Adlai Stevenson down to his toes. He might as well have little Bolsheviks pumping his heart, running out on his tongue, and waving a red flag. You know what he said the other day? Wants to end the draft."

Ira sat on the edge of his bed, slipping his stockinged feet into shiny black pants. "The Communists have enough trouble of their own without taking on ours," he said. "Poland and Hungary."

"That's just why they want to take over this country!" Henry Parker spat into an empty macaroni can kept by his bed for that purpose. "They need our spirit, our know-how. Our money. But it doesn't matter because the Republicans are going to win. That's the one thing Emit doesn't understand. He doesn't appreciate the power of the Republicans, even in Texas. He thinks the country's already been sold down the river."

Mr. Parker vigorously rubbed a generous amount of Brylcreem into his scalp. "What kind of name is Adlai anyway? Might be a Russian name for all we know. I never heard of it." He turned away from the mirror. "Do I look all right, Ira? I mean, is there anything hanging out?"

"No, Henry. You look fine."

"Well, we might as well be on our way," Mr. Parker declared.

"I wonder if there will be dancing," he said as they started down the hall. "I don't know how the church would feel about that sort of thing. Do you dance, Ira?"

"No. I never learned."

Mr. Parker stopped in the doorway of the community room. He straightened Ira's tie affectionately. "You probably never learned because you never married. It makes me sad, Ira. It makes me sad to think that you missed so much."

Kathleen wore a dress that matched the green and gold flowers on the refreshment table and the twisted crepe paper overhead. It was her brightest dress, and if a little hot for the season, made her feel gay. Her heavy hair was pulled higher up on her head than usual. "Who is giving this party?" she asked.

"The Baptist Church biddies," Azzie answered. "That's what I call them."

"Who is it for? Are you certain it is all right that I come?"

"For? Why, it's for us, who do you think? And we deserve it, too."

"But they don't even know us," Kathleen persisted, perplexed by the roomful of strangers. "Or at least they don't know me."

"I'd keep it that way," Azzie advised. She pressed on Kathleen's arm. "Do you see food anywhere?"

Kathleen nodded. "Yes, on a table in the center."

"They always have food!" Azzie exclaimed gleefully. "It's the only time we get a decent meal. I wonder if they have those little chocolate cookies they had last time." She grinned broadly. "My God, they were good."

A quartet from the India High School led by an acned and lanky flutist began to play "Star Dust" and several married couples from town decided to dance. Kathleen led Azzie to one of the steel chairs lining the wall. Azzie arranged herself comfortably and pulled Kathleen close to her, whispering in her ear. In compliance with her request, Kathleen dodged the dancers and headed for the refreshment table.

Andrew Carlyle watched all this from the opposite side of the room, where he sat alone. He recognized Azzie when she came in and he grew expectant, but Jimi June did not follow, only some woman he did not know. There had been a great deal of nibbling and milling around before the music started, and it was after eight now. She was not coming, he decided. Just as she had not appeared for any meal since dinner five nights before.

He had finally asked about her that afternoon. The possibility that she was ill had occupied his mind during the past half week; once or twice he had even considered that she might be dead. Certainly no one would think to tell him. The aide or the nurse, whatever she was, he had stopped in the hallway was a bit annoyed at his questions. She assured him that Jimi June was "not at all ill," but added with a frown that flattened her wide nose, "Miss Hasbrook is not in a mood to leave her room."

Thinking of this exchange, Mr. Carlyle stuffed some cookies he had been holding into the pocket of his pants and left the community room. He was determined to see Jimi June after squeezing himself into a suit he hadn't worn in years and appearing at a silly affair, all for the purpose of determining that she was indeed not ill. A mood could mean anything to a woman of her age, especially a woman who had been locked away for decades. Once or twice he had caught something in her face— youth, expectancy, nerve. A mood could mean anything.

She did not answer his knock. He pushed the door open and the vague moist scent of a short confinement rushed out. "Hello," he called.

She moved.

"What are you doing in here in the dark?" he demanded, directing himself toward the sound. "Are you sick? What is wrong with you?"

"Carlyle?"

"Where are you?"

"Leave me alone, Carlyle!"

"What is the matter with you? Where's the light?"

"Go away! No!" she cried shrilly when she heard him bump into the table where a lamp was.

It took a moment for his eyes to adjust to the light, and he heard her before he could make out her form. He was closer to her than he would have guessed.

She slapped at him and caught the far side of his cheek.

"Don't." He backed away. "Who did this to you?"

Jimi June shook her head furiously. She would not look at him.

"Wait a minute." Andrew turned off the light and found her again in the dark. "Give me your hand, Jimi. . . ."

"You shouldn't stay in here by yourself," he said after a moment.

He could barely understand her reply. "They told me not to go out."

"Who told you?" He pressed her hand. "One of the aides? Mrs. Johnston?"

She nodded violently.

"That bitch," he muttered. "Did she do this to you?"

Jimi June did not answer.

"You know"—he spoke gently—"there was a little blind boy who lived next door to Angie and me for a time. He was a quiet little boy, never said much, and one day he took a pair of scissors to his hair. He didn't leave too much more than you have now, but it didn't bother him any because he couldn't see it and it was cool for him in the summertime. It was a hot summer that year, I remember, just like this one. And by the time the winter came his hair was all grown out thicker than before. That's the thing about hair. It will always grow back." He laughed shortly. "At least for you and that little neighbor boy. It's me you should be worrying about. Did you see that bald spot on the top of my head? I'll tell you, it keeps me up nights."

"Carlyle?"

"Yes, Jimi."

"How are you, Carlyle?"

"I would be just fine if I didn't have to think about your foolishness. Here." He reached into his pants pocket with his free hand. "I picked these up for you."

"What are they?"

"Cookies."

"Lemon?"

"Chocolate. I couldn't find any saltines. They almost didn't have any of these, the way your roommate was going after them."

Jimi June took a bite. "How many have you got?"

"Three."

"She cries," Jimi June said after a moment.

"Who is that?"

"My roommate."

"What do you mean? Is she sick?"

"Her daughter and her husband died. Thank you for the cookies, Carlyle."

Andrew moved his hand to the back of her bristled head. "Are you determined to sit in this black corner?"

"They won't let me go out."

"Well." He thought for a moment. "I guess I'll just stay here with you for a while."

Henry Parker enjoyed seeing people from town, but tonight the news was mostly about people he did not know. Some Lovall Stranger or Stronger had been promoted at the Clerk's Office, and a new insurance office had opened on Pritchett Street, four blocks from the central square and thought to be a poor location. Mr. Parker had a pleasant conversation with Jason Hadley's son, Castor, who was interested in selling his chain of gas stations and going into banking, but their discussion had been interrupted about five minutes ago when Castor's wife came up to get him for a dance.

Mr. Parker took two of three remaining tea sandwiches from the refreshment table. What sort of pretension or prejudice would motivate someone to cut the crust off a perfectly good piece of bread, he wondered, popping the second sandwich into his mouth. He toyed with the idea of finishing the last one to make up for their mean size, but just at that moment he caught sight of Azzie Bowdin's companion.

Kathleen was sitting silently and straight in one of the steel chairs while Azzie dozed with her head on Kathleen's shoulder. At one point in the past half hour, Kathleen had gently awakened her and offered to help her to bed, but Azzie insisted that she wanted to stay until the very end. "I'm just full from the cookies." She had smiled lazily. "They make me sleepy."

Mr. Parker vaguely remembered Ira mentioning that there was a new woman, but that had been almost the beginning of the summer. It seemed impossible to Mr. Parker that he would not have seen her in all this time unless she were ancient or very ill. This woman was not, although she did have a certain frailty about her. Much thinner than the other women at the home, and with a certain clear paleness to her skin.

It was a silly schoolboy gesture, Henry Parker told himself the instant he had the sandwich in his hand, but he was already walking toward her and had caught her attention. "Do you want this sandwich?" he asked while still quite a distance away.

She gave no response and he waited until he was closer. "Do you want this sandwich?"

"No; thank you anyway," she replied in a voice that would not disturb Azzie. "I have already had one."

Mr. Parker was standing in front of her. "No? Well, can't let it go to waste; it's the last one." He held it above his open mouth. "Sure?"

"Thank you anyway."

"I guess I will have to eat it myself." He laughed too loudly and dropped it whole into his mouth.

Azzie opened one eye. "Who's that?" she demanded, seeing a life-size form in front of her.

"Hello, Azalea," Mr. Parker mumbled through bread crumbs.

"Jason Hadley, is that you?" She giggled. "You old jackass. Couldn't stay away."

"It's Henry Parker."

"Well, Henry, hello!" Azzie returned just as cheerfully. "I was wondering if any eligible men were going to pay attention to us. Some party, don't you think?"

"Yes, I say."

"Did you get any of those chocolate cookies?"

"They were fine," he agreed, impatient.

"What have you been doing with yourself, Henry? I never see you around. Course, I never see anybody." Azzie wrinkled her nose. "I just smell them."

"Not too much," Mr. Parker replied, and stole a look at Kathleen. "I thought perhaps your friend might like to dance."

"Oh, no. Oh, no, thank you."

Azzie pushed Kathleen's shoulder. "Why, sure, honey. You're not so old; you ought to go ahead. Don't worry about me. Lord knows I would be out there if I weren't so blind. And fat!" She covered her mouth. "I'm getting fat, Henry."

"I can't dance." Kathleen addressed Henry Parker.

"That's no problem," he assured her. "All you have to do is follow."

"No." She played with her dress nervously. "I meant, I know how to dance, or at least I used to. I am married." She looked away shyly.

"That's the truth," Azzie affirmed. "Mrs. Storrs is her name. Have you been introduced? Mrs. Storrs, Mr. Parker. Phillip is her husband's name, Phillip Storrs. She is waiting for Phillip to come and get her, take her home. He will be coming any day now."

"Oh." Mr. Parker nodded. A wet belch ran up his throat and he caught it, stammering his words. "That's wonderful. I didn't know." He backed away. "Good to see you both."

His forehead burned. "I am a damned fool," Mr. Parker admonished himself. He wished for Margaret Helen. If she were still with him, he would not do such silly things. But she was not, and Henry Parker searched the room for his friend. Ira, too, was gone.

Ira fell onto his bed, pressing his trembling hands into his armpits. They knocked weakly at his ribs. He rolled over, trying to push himself deeper into the bed. He was cold.

This was the worst it had been, he knew. A slight quivering was all it had been before, or a shudder he attributed to a draft after his bath or an open window. Tonight it had started just that way, a slight movement in his fingertips (he was drinking a cup of punch at the party) that spread like a biting flame up his arms to his head until he felt his tongue move. The glass left his hand, he dragged his head from side to side, half hoping he had alerted the whole room, half hoping to hide a fit that threatened to throw him onto the floor where he placed his foot, again and again, neatly raking the pieces of glass far under his chair.

Ira turned his head into the pillow. He was remembering the last hour, sliding himself along the wall toward his room, falling down in front of open doors that offered no support. "Like a snake" had flashed through his mind.

It was stopping now, like violent wind, and he closed his eyes. Sarah's smile was not quite straight, he thought, and tried to look at it more closely. One corner spread upward; she was amused by his game and he laughed, too, short, breathless gasps at his grandiose scene. She sang a brief song in return.

It was raining outside. Through the pillow he could hear it on the glass pane. Sarah was always content to play inside in weather like this.

CHAPTER 12

No one ever determined exactly what the Phillipses had decided: that their mother, Vidy, was recently dead inside her room in Fulton Hall, or that her demise was imminent, or perhaps just that the time seemed ripe and they hoped their loaded presence would serve to speed nature on her course. Some sort of reasoning brought the entire family, including the two sons, Steven and Troy Daniel, their wives and children, a cousin, Marguerite, and an ancient uncle who remembered Vidy as a girl, before all the trouble started, to the gates of the state hospital on Saturday, the tenth of September. They were towing a casket in their station wagon and carrying the deed to a burial plot and the receipt for a dozen mixed carnations and thirty-six gladiolas arranged in a small horseshoe wreath. Whatever their thinking or prophecy, it was shot when the registrar at the main desk could find no one by the name of V. Phillips on her roll books. After inquiring at several of the newer wards, the registrar reached the nurse at Fulton, who conveyed the information that Vidy Phillips, alive and alert, had been transferred ten months earlier to a nursing home in India.

From Valorda to India is a distance of seventy miles, and it was after seven when the makeshift hearse pulled into the parking lot of Twilight Days. The residents had finished with a light supper an hour earlier and most were napping in their rooms, anticipating the night's sleep. A few television sets were turned to "Talent Scouts." Vidy Phillips was in 16A, helping her roommate, Becky Springer, select her fall garden, when Frances Crawford, the evening aide for their ward, interrupted them.

"Mrs. Crawford," Becky cawed. "Do you know if sweet potatoes do well in the shade? We hardly get any sunlight over here. I don't see why they don't move me to the other side of the hall."

"I think sweet potatoes do best without too much sun," Mrs. Crawford answered. "I'll ask my husband." She turned to Vidy. "Vidy," she began casually, "I didn't know you had a family."

"Oh, yes." Vidy worked her tongue. "I've got two sons, a husband, three brothers, and some dogs. We used to have a big old dog at home, one of them hairy ones."

Mrs. Crawford was cautious. "I guess you haven't seen your family in some time."

"Well, I was thinking that maybe the girl down the hall might be a cousin of mine, but I wasn't sure."

"Well, some of them are here tonight."

"They are?" Vidy giggled. "Tell them to come in if they want. Reckon they know anything about sweet potatoes?"

Steven Phillips was the first to come in. He introduced

himself formally and dutifully informed his mother of her husband's death some eight years before.

"I'm sorry to hear that, sure sorry," Vidy responded politely. "Was it his kidneys?"

"No, ma'am, his heart."

Vidy shrugged. "I didn't ever know anything about his heart." She turned to Becky. "Kidneys used to make his arm swell up."

The door opened and Uncle J.E. burst into the room. "I couldn't wait any longer," he proclaimed, a wiry, seemingly jointless old man. "Ohhhh," he laughed. "Nobody has to tell me—this is my little Vidy." Troy Daniel, Marguerite, the wives and children followed him in file, and Vidy greeted each one warmly. Uncle J.E. soon lapsed into a monologue on the days when he was younger, which loosely included Vidy, and it was after ten when Becky Springer declared she had heard enough and Mrs. Crawford more tactfully suggested that they might call it a night. Marguerite, the wives, and Uncle J.E. took a room in the City Motel, and the remainder of the group slept in the car around the coffin or on the grass beside the motel. They left after a brief visit with Vidy in the morning, calling out of the car windows promises to send Steven back the following Friday to carry Vidy to Waketon for the weekend.

"You're late."

"Yes, I know." Monica Whitwell lowered her eyes, lovely eyes, the color of a century plant. It was four-thirty on Friday afternoon. "I had some typing to finish. But look what I've brought you." She held up a white paper bag. "I stopped by the bakery."

Her father ignored her.

"Pecan sandies. I don't know if they are still your favorites, but I never knew you to turn one down."

"You don't think I get enough starch and junk around here?" Dr. Whitwell demanded. "Potatoes and bread is what they feed us, you know."

"I thought you might like something sweet for a change."

"You look like you've been eating them."

"Papa."

"It just irritates me, Monica." He pushed himself up in the bed. "You have no regard for my work. It seems perfectly fine to you to spend the afternoon typing for some jerk selling mobile homes instead of being on time to help your father. God knows, I wouldn't ask you unless I absolutely had to."

"I have to make a living," she answered him softly.

"You ought to get married. Oh, hell." He shook his head. "It's no use discussing it with you. Do you at least have some paper ready?"

"Yes."

"All right. I was talking about Mrs. Drachmore. I want to continue with her. Read me the last sentence."

Monica opened her loose-leaf notebook. " 'I was able to relieve the pressure on the third and fourth thoracic nerves.' "

"Yes." He nodded. "I was. Now get this down: I was able to do that by daily rotating the muscle tissue and giving deep massage for a period of three weeks. I was also careful to keep the area stimulated by heat. . . . Monica." He interrupted his dictation. "Very few people are educated to that principle. Other doctors had given

Mrs. Drachmore no hope to ever walk again without pain, possibly a limp for the rest of her life. You've seen her around town. She could outrace you or anyone else. Hasn't felt a wince of pain since she finished with my treatment."

"I know, Papa. You have done some remarkable things."

"Nobody ever called me a quack!"

"No."

"They wouldn't dare. The proof is all around them." He was silent for several minutes. She held her pencil ready. "There are very few men," he said finally, "who can look back at their life's work as I can, meet their accomplishments on the street. But they won't always be alive to testify. That's why this book is so important." He was watching her intensely. "Can you understand that, Monica?"

"Yes, yes, of course I can. I'm sorry, Papa, I . . ."

Dr. Whitwell moved his hand under the bedspread and squeezed one of his crippled legs. "There was never anybody who could help me. It doesn't seem quite fair."

"You have been very brave since the accident."

"I don't have time for this," he answered, gruff again. "Let's go on to Patrick Waterhouse. This is number two hundred and three."

For her first trip home, Vidy was dressed in a light-blue cotton dress that fell to her midshin, and short socks in a lighter shade. She carried a heavy-knit red sweater and a black vinyl handbag. A green yarn ribbon tickled her earlobe and she slapped at it absently. "I am going home," she reminded Becky Springer.

"You told me. What time are they coming after you?" she queried in her uneven voice.

"This afternoon. I am going to spend the weekend with them. We are going to make ice cream. That's what Miss Henrietta said. She said we probably would." Vidy gave her chin a quick bath. "You know how the salt gets down in there and tears your dress up? Tears your dress all up and then it ain't no good. And along comes a little kitty and gets in there. Or a little doggy; either one." She giggled happily.

"I used to make ice cream," Becky recalled.

"Yeah, it's good." Vidy opened her purse for the fourth time in as many minutes. She studied the lining and the thin zipper running along the side. "I hope I got everything."

"Your suitcase is jammed full."

"I think I do. I guess if I forgot my radio or anything, they would have one. Don't you reckon?"

Becky had lost interest in the conversation, and Vidy settled back in her chair, admiring her suitcase and bag. This was the most fun she could remember having since Mrs. Risner at the state hospital had let her help with the Christmas party one year. Of course, it was work, too, Vidy acknowledged and closed her eyes, tired from her preparations. She had never done any work, except it seemed to her that once she had picked some cotton, but it had been a long while. Remembering made her even more drowsy, and in a few moments her grip on her purse loosened and her head fell back.

The summer has gone, Mr. Parker thought, moved on like a blanket of crows down toward Mexico, the hot wind blowing on the arid flat land like the flapping of a thousand greedy wings. It was still warm but the sweltering flush of the season had passed over. The weather would be nothing to talk of until winter.

The change left him fatigued, but then he was always sleepy on afternoons like this when he had the porch to himself. Adam was absorbed in his book and Uncle Robert, too, had complained of tiredness earlier and gone inside for a nap. Two weeks ago Mr. Parker would have done the same, but nowadays he preferred to be out of the room. At night, of course, there was no place else to go, and he would lie awake listening to Ira giggle and talk to someone in a strange soprano voice. It was the medication, the doctor had assured Mr. Parker when he asked.

He yawned and stretched his body open to the breeze. This weather lets you alone, he thought. Mr. Parker was new to the feeling of a light wind playing around his body. It was not like the short gusts sent down several times a minute by the three-pronged ceiling fan that had rotated above his desk in the bank, nor like the air cooler when they finally got it. More like the end of a long bath, Henry Parker decided, the time when there is no difference between the feel of air and water, before the chill sets in. Mr. Parker closed his eyes. He heard the rustle of the first brown fallen leaves on the parking lot, and some children far in the distance. In this way the afternoon slowly passed, Henry Parker keeping himself just in front of sleep in case someone from town should happen by. But the only visitor was a stranger. He came in last year's Chevrolet station wagon.

"Vidy." Bess Turner shook her gently. "Your son is here. Steven is here to take you home. Wake up, Vidy."

Vidy opened her eyes and collected her tongue. "What?"

Steven Phillips was a large man who carried his weight with good humor and confidence, not at all in the way he had as a youth. "Hello, Mother." He grinned easily.

"What did you say?" Vidy addressed Mrs. Turner.

"Are your things packed?" Bess Turner wondered. "You have quite a distance to go and it is after four now. The traffic will be heavy around C. City if you don't get started."

"Are you ready, Mother?" Steven tried to take her hand.

"Who are you?" Vidy demanded indignantly.

"Vidy, what do you mean?" Mrs. Turner glanced at Steven Phillips apologetically. "She's just a little confused, being awakened like that."

"It's all right." Steven crouched in front of Vidy. "Mother." He spoke quietly and Vidy listened. "Don't you remember last Saturday when I came to see you and brought Troy Daniel and the grandchildren? Do you remember Troy Daniel?"

She shook her head.

"Troy Daniel is your other son. He is waiting for you at our home in Waketon. I am going to take you there for a visit."

Vidy took a moment to consider the proposition. "I don't want to go."

"I don't understand, Vidy," Mrs. Turner said, imitating Steven's patient tone. "You have been so excited all week, and look, here is your bag all packed and you are dressed to go. You look so pretty."

"I am tired," Vidy answered.

"I will bring you back on Sunday," Steven promised.

Vidy stroked her lips. "You are going to take me to that fair and leave me."

"What are you talking about?" Steven wondered out loud. "It is too early for the fair."

"Don't you remember when we went with all those people? We walked so far and everybody looked so nice, all white and pretty, and they dressed us up, too." Vidy laughed. "I had a pink polka dot dress but they gave me another one. But I don't want to go with you now. I have to help Becky with her sweet potatoes."

"You can help Becky on Monday," he suggested. "Maybe I can even find some cuttings and seeds for you to bring back. Becky would like that." He placed his arm around her thick shoulders. "Let's go home now."

"I don't know you," Vidy complained. "This is my home."

"Just for the weekend, Mother."

"Don't call me that!" She rolled back her tongue with remembered accuracy. "Now leave me alone."

Bess Turner hurried him out, offering him a Kleenex to wipe his face. Vidy seemed to have forgotten the incident when she returned a few minutes later and began slowly to unpack the bulging suitcase. "Miss Bess," Vidy asked politely, "are they bringing that black jam with dinner? You know, the kind with the little bugs in it? I hope not, 'cause they always get down in my teeth."

"Mine, too," Becky Springer echoed.

CHAPTER 13

"Where have you been?" Ira demanded.

"At school."

"But it is after five. What have you been doing?"

"Playing."

"Playing? Playing with whom?"

"Some kids." She turned her head.

"All alone? You shouldn't play all alone, Sarah. It is very dangerous. All kinds of things might happen to you. A fall."

"Billy was there."

"I have been waiting for two hours, Sarah. It was a beautiful day and I thought—Sarah! What are you doing in that corner?"

"What is the name of your mother's boyfriend?"

"Alex."

"Alex." Ira laughed. "Sounds like a dandy."

"I don't like him."

"She is going out with him on Friday night and you are going to stay here with me. Won't that be fun?"

She pulled her black hair into a single tight curl. "Can we have a TV dinner?" She looked older.

"What are you doing in that corner?" he demanded. "You are going to get black as thunder."

She sat in an oil spill on the far side of his garage.

"I wanted to go to the woods or to the park," Ira continued. "We still have an hour before your dinnertime. I'll get my sweater."

"I don't want to go." Sarah wrapped her toe with a piece of string like a mummy.

"And what else is red?"

"Beans."

He nodded. "Some beans. And apples—how about them?"

"Your cup."

"Yes, my cup is red."

"Roses." She was hesitant with the name.

"That's right, roses. And what are roses? Your mother is not here yet, Sarah. She and Alex have gone to a party. I told you they were going and it would be late when they got home."

She threw out her arms and whirled. "I want to go home! I want to go home!"

"Are you sleepy?"

"Yes."

"You can sleep here. I will take you upstairs and you can lie down on my bed."

Sarah had made a nail fence around her. She folded and sat on her colt legs. "I don't want to go."

"You don't want to go to the forest? It is your favorite walk."

She looked around his garage for another plaything. "No."

"Well." He did not understand her mood. "Would you like to come inside? I think I have some mints."

She ignored him fiercely.

"Do you want to just sit there?" He tried to tease.

She ran the piece of string between her naked toes, raising her hand high so that she bent with the length of it. She gave a cry.

"Sarah! What is it? Are you ill?"

"We are going away."

"And tomatoes and pomegranates and Mrs. Kelsey's garage down the block. What else?"

"Strawberries are red."

"Um hum."

"Alex's face."

"Is it red? All the time, or when he is mad?"

"All the time. Every day, every hour, every minute, every"—she hesitated—"minute," she repeated.

"Ants," Ira suggested.

She raised ten fingers curled toward him. "Snow with blood!"

"I think that would be pink," he answered.

"I didn't mean to wake you," he whispered.

She bolted. "Is my mother here?"

"No. She called, and I told her you were sleeping and she said not to wake you. She will see you in the morning."

"I want to go home."

"Are you afraid of the dark, Sarah?"

She threw off the covers he had arranged.

"Don't be frightened. Please, Sarah, I can turn on the light. You know I wouldn't let anything hurt you. I wouldn't hurt you. I wasn't going to stay in here. Is it the dark, Sarah? I was going to sleep downstairs."

"What do you mean, you are going away?"

She breathed the word into his stomach. "Moving."

He said nothing.

"To a big state," she clarified.

"When?"

"Next week."

"Is Alex going?" The thought had just occurred to him.

She nodded. "I don't remember when."

"I thought you said next week."

"I don't remember."

"It hardly matters."

Jason Hadley had always been a slow walker, or perhaps leisurely would be more accurate, for as he shuffled along he liked to stop and visit with the people he knew, which still included most of the citizens of India, or sit on any curb and watch the people he didn't. Today he was particularly slothful because Azzie's request had sent him two blocks out of his way, and when he returned to the home there was a go fish game in progress in the lobby that caught his attention. Jason had known Fronie MacDermott from the time they went to grammar school together in Mercedes, a town about six miles from India.

He positioned himself behind Fronie where he could see her hand. She was holding two queens, three sevens, a deuce, and a pair of nines.

"Do you have any eights?" Dorothy Tyler demanded.

"What?" Fronie stretched her fleshy ear. "What did she say?"

"Eights!" Jason Hadley cried.

"Eights," Mrs. Tyler repeated. "Do you have any eights?"

"No."

"Are you sure? You certainly came up with a ten mighty fast a few minutes ago, just two turns after I had asked you for one."

"Of course I am sure." Her opponent huffed at the implication. "I haven't seen an eight this whole game. Go fishing."

It was Fronie's turn. "Do you have any twos?"

"Here."

"Only one?"

"Don't complain."

"How about sevens?"

Dorothy Tyler shook her head and smiled viciously. "Give me your queens," she ordered.

"You don't mean it!"

"I just drew one. Hand the ladies over."

Fronie surrendered the cards. "You are so far ahead I shall never catch up."

"Do you have any fours?" Mrs. Tyler replied.

Azzie was standing in her doorway tapping her cane furiously when Jason finally made his way to her room. "Hello there, Azalea," he called.

"Where the hell have you been?"

"I'm sorry." He reached her. "I had to wait for Bristol to finish distributing the late mail."

"What did he say?"

"He said that there was no mail for you, and that all the mail is picked up in the mornings anyway. That is true. Mrs. Johnston gets it before she comes in."

Azzie turned abruptly and walked back into her room. "She is a thief!"

Jason Hadley scratched the back of his hand and followed her.

"She is stealing my letters. This proves it."

"Now, Azalea, you must be getting pretty interesting letters for someone to want to take them. The mail is so slow nowadays you probably just haven't gotten it yet."

"No, it has been weeks. Nothing from Mr. Roscoe?" she asked. "Nothing from the Welfare Department, the Shriners?" Azzie tried to remember the list of epistles she had dictated to Mrs. Zeagler in the past week. "Help for the Handicapped?"

He shook his head.

"Well?"

"No," he answered.

"They are keeping my letters. I'm telling you, they are keeping my letters because they don't want me to leave."

"I don't—"

Azzie swung her cane in front of her wildly. "I'm not going to stay here!"

"Azalea."

"Get out of here, Jason."

He turned in the doorway. "I'm sorry there wasn't any mail for you, Azalea. Why don't you come down to the dining room tonight and sit with me at dinner?"

"No." She was thinking. "You can bring me a piece of fruit or a cookie. For my friend. But that's all I want from you. Now go on." She turned her back to him.

Ira stretched his legs the full length of the bed. He had just been sponged and dressed in fresh pajamas, and he felt much calmer. He spoke more quietly.

"Sarah," he proposed. "Are you certain that it is not just a trip? Perhaps they are taking you with them on their honeymoon. Or not taking you at all. Maybe you are to stay here with me. That seems likely. You will not be frightened this time, will you?"

She shook her head solemnly. "The moving truck is coming," she said.

"I see."

"I will stay with you!" she proclaimed. "We can move all my things before it comes. Jody"—she began with her favorite cloth toy—"and Essie and Charly and my squirrel."

"Yes," he replied, absorbed with the weight of her on his knee. "I don't see how."

"We can do it."

"No." He was not talking to her but to a cluster of small wood blocks on the far side of his garage. "I suppose you must go with your mother. They make you do that. The courts, I mean."

"I don't want to leave you!"

"Yes. Well." He was shamefully aware of the tears collecting in his eyes. "We are friends, aren't we?"

"My best friend."

"Your best friend," he repeated. "That is quite a lot.

I suppose"—he was timid—"I suppose you shall still have me as a friend."

"My best friend!"

"I shall still be your best friend. And you mine." Ira raised the small face. He was surprised. "Don't cry, Sarah."

"But I won't see you anymore."

"Of course we will. Best friends always see each other again."

She was doubtful; she held his legs, one hand loosely tucked under his knee.

"Is the big state far away?"

"Uh huh."

"Is it in the north or east or where?"

"I don't remember."

"California," he guessed.

She shook her head. Perhaps.

"Next week doesn't seem like time enough to get ready."

"It is cold there."

"Where?"

"Alex said it was cold in the state."

Ira nodded.

He did not seem very interested and she moved away, finding the familiar piece of string. "I am going home." She did not move.

"Home? Already? But, Sarah . . ."

"You will find another friend."

"No!"

She came up on her knees. "I have seen you before."

"What do you mean?"

"I saw." Her finger toyed with her mouth, coaxing the words. "Who was that little girl who was here last week?" She had phrased it as though it were only curiosity.

"That was the daughter of a lady who sometimes helps me out at the newspaper. Mrs. Railey. You probably know that little girl: Anne. She is a grade ahead of you, I think."

"What was she doing here? Her mother wasn't here."

"Her mother had to visit someone in the hospital."

"She is not your friend?"

"Anne? She is a very nice child, but no, not in the way you mean. She is not my friend."

"She won't be your friend when I go?"

"No. And you? What about Alex?"

"I don't like him."

"But you will. After you get to know him. Children always do, it seems."

"I won't."

"It is all right if you do."

"I won't!"

"Do you promise like I did?" Ira was hopeful.

"I will prove it!" Her eyes were bright. "We will take an oath."

He was caught by the tone of her eyes. "What is that?"

"Do you have a pin?"

She ran to a squatty set of drawers where he kept his gardening equipment and what tools he had thought to acquire over his life.

"A pin? You mean a straight pin?"

"Any kind."

"I believe I have a safety pin somewhere in here." He opened the top drawer. "What do you need a safety pin for?" he asked, handing her one.

"For the blood."

"For the blood! Sarah! What do you mean?"

She giggled, excited, cheered. "You have to punch your finger and get blood," she instructed. "And then I punch my finger and get my blood. It doesn't hurt, only a little. And then we rub them together."

"What does that do?" He was intrigued but tired and sat on a discarded living room chair. "I am getting old, Sarah," he muttered.

"It makes us blood brothers so that no one can take my place."

"But no one will."

"We have to do this," she insisted with her foot.

"Sarah."

"I will go away and get another friend if we don't."

Ira agreed.

"You go first," she said.

He opened the pin.

"You're scared." She pushed him. "I will do it," she said. "Let me have it."

Ira raised it above his hand.

"In your finger," she directed.

He jabbed.

"Let me have it," she cried.

"You don't have to do it," he assured her. "I did it. That is enough. Isn't that enough, Sarah?" He held out his bleeding finger.

She touched the point of the pin into her middle finger. "It didn't do."

"It doesn't matter. I did it. Give me back the pin."

She closed her eyes and stabbed, tearing the skin.

"Hurry!" she screamed, biting the wounded tip. "Before the blood dries!"

"You're hurt!"

"Get the blood!"

Her finger felt hot under his. She made a smeared series of lines down to the inside of his knuckle. "I promise," she declared with serious eyes, "I will not take Alex for my best friend."

"And you will always be my best friend." Ira could smell the blood.

It was not enough. "Say you will never take Anne Railey for your best friend."

"I won't ever."

"The blood is all dry."

"We will see each other again."

CHAPTER 14

She had found nothing in Ima Johnston's drawer. Letters certainly—the drawer was filled with envelopes addressed in tiny or careless hands that were impossible for Azzie to make out. They might have been for her; she would never know. Her failed eyes enraged her; equally the coward Miss Zeagler, who had at the last minute feigned illness and refused to help. But Azzie was not thinking of any of these matters while she sat, resigned to the prospect of jail or, worse, the asylum. Her hands were quiet and they lay loosely in her lap.

She was thinking of Peggy. Azzie could not understand why Peggy no longer loved her. Certainly she had at one time, when she was a girl clinging to her mother in stores and crying out for her in the night, lonesome. Even after Peggy had married, and after Harry died, she came two or three times a year to see her mother and always at Christmas. Azzie could remember no incident or declaration which would have changed all that. Something must have been said that Azzie had forgotten. Had she denounced Peggy in a moment of warmth? Embarrassed her, perhaps, laughed at her cruelly? There must be something standing between them. Peggy would not do this otherwise. Azzie wiped at her wet face. Perhaps Peggy had come after all and Azzie had not seen her, not realized. Her eyes failed her so.

By dusk Azzie's hips and legs were sore from their one position, and the drowsiness, which had been flirting with her since midafternoon, began to win its way. Her dinner came and she ate the meat from it and a small bowl of vanilla ice cream. It seemed after all that the police were not coming for her. She maneuvered herself from the chair to her bed. No one was coming for her.

"Daddy?"

"Daddy?"

Earl Brogdon's eyes remained closed.

"Daddy, I have to talk to you."

"I am sleeping," he murmured.

"I know, Daddy. I am sorry to disturb you, but this is important. Can you open your eyes, Daddy?"

A hand was slipped under Earl's cheek. "I am sleeping, I tell you!"

"Come on, get up. We are going to take a little walk."

He flashed open his gray eyes. "Clay." He addressed a fair, open-faced man. His oldest son.

"I need to talk to you." Clay grasped his father's shoulders and pulled him upright. "You are dressed," he announced, surprised. "I thought you were sleeping."

"I just lay down for a nap," Earl started to explain but was propelled to his feet. "Where are you taking me?"

"You need a sweater."

"Outside?"

148

"For a walk, Daddy."

"I don't want to go." Earl pulled away from the open sleeve held for him.

"I have something to tell you," Clay said quietly.

"What? About your mother?" Earl questioned anxiously. "Does she still have her cold?"

"No. Not about Mother. She is fine. Now, please, Daddy."

Earl walked nervously and slowly; like an old cat on a wire fence, he tediously placed one foot in front of the other along the lines of the tiles. Clay tried to measure his own steps, but long before the front door was reached, he had changed to taking discreet pauses. When his father got far enough ahead, Clay would make one normal move.

"It's hot out here," Earl complained, pulling at his wool sweater.

"Not really so hot since Labor Day." He led Earl beyond the porch. "Mother had quite a time protecting her face from the sun this summer."

Earl stopped in front of a large rock.

"Here, let me help you."

"No." He shook off his son's arm. "I can make it. How is your mother? She didn't get burned, I hope." Earl tried to sound a bit casual. "She has such fair skin." He maneuvered around the rock with the stilted movements of a windup toy rounding a plastic mountain.

"She is fine, Daddy."

"Does she ask about me?"

"All the time," Clay lied.

"Where are we going?"

"Let's sit here."

They were on top of the hill that began D. Byrd Case's pasture. Earl lowered himself carefully to sit on a squatty piece of wood near the edge.

Clay sat close to his father. "Ellen and the children are fine," he told him, referring to his own family.

"What did you bring me out here for?" his father demanded. Last time he had looked out, the world had been darker and more lively. The green had soured into tan.

"How are you feeling, Father?"

"Fine," he answered impatiently.

Clay traced a distant spotted cow with his finger. "Do you remember that appointment you had with the doctor in C. City?"

"What? Yes, of course."

"I had a call from that doctor the other day."

Earl said nothing. He played with pebbles nervously.

"Yesterday, in fact. It seems he took an x-ray while you were there, because you were complaining of that pain in your ear. Anyway, the results came back"—Clay rolled a stick down the grassless hill bank—"and he phoned me. He has found something, Daddy."

"What do you mean, something? What kind of something?"

"A little knot. He's not sure." Clay lowered his voice.

"What?" It was sharp, insistent, scared.

"A tumor."

"Cancer," Earl clarified.

"No!" Clay protested. "He doesn't know what it is. He can't know until he does some more tests. But you will have to go to the hospital in C. City. I will take you there myself."

"Does your mother know?"

He nodded.

"It is in my ear." He pressed an uneven pebble into his palm.

"Yeah. That is what he said."

Earl pushed himself up to standing. "What did you bring me out here for?"

"I had to tell you about this. I thought you would want to be alone when you heard."

"I am not alone," Earl replied with disdain, pushing the pebble deeper into his palm. He stepped back.

"Daddy, be careful!"

Earl encountered the hill—a sudden surprise behind him. His stout feet turned in and out uncertainly, and Earl joined his gray stone's fall into the landscape, the gravel dirt and oak trees.

Ira delivered another spoonful of softened toast and cream of wheat to his mouth and stared at the narrow white band taped to his glass of milk. "IS–4C," handwritten with pastel pencil, followed by the stamped slogan: "Daisy Fresh Makes Healthy Men." Ira took a sip. This was the first morning in a half month that his breakfast had not been a shot that by nine o'clock left his veins and nerves collapsed and floating with his blood. The food felt thick in his mouth, and he ate slowly, ignoring the pill waiting beside his plate, a replacement package of certain laziness.

"Henry!" he called cheerfully as his roommate came through the door. He pushed himself up in the bed.

"Hello," Henry Parker returned, pleased but with an overtone of hesitancy. "How are you feeling?"

"Much better, Henry, thank you. How are you?"

"Well," Mr. Parker answered. "I am well." He glanced at Ira's hand.

"I am better, Henry."

"I guess all this sleep has been good for you."

"How is everyone?"

"Fine." Mr. Parker nodded. "You know Meredith Fulbright passed away?"

"No!"

"I guess you were—" He stopped and rephrased his words. "A week or two ago. They've already had the funeral."

"I am so sorry to hear about that. I knew her husband."

"I heard it was a fine funeral."

"How is Uncle Robert? The doctor?"

"The same."

"Has Adam finished his book?"

Mr. Parker chuckled and stretched out on his bed. "He has to run out of breath first."

Ira studied the amount of light coming through the curtains. "The weather seems good," he remarked.

"It's muggy still."

"No rain?"

"No. We need it again."

"I'm just as glad," Ira said and pushed his cool breakfast aside. "I don't want Sarah to have to travel in it."

"Sarah? Sarah who?"

"Sarah Aberdeen. Is it the weekend yet, Henry? I imagine she will come on the weekend."

Henry Parker sat up, remembering Ira's strange talk in the night.

"She insisted on coming to see me the moment she heard I was ill."

"Ira." Mr. Parker worked to control his voice. "How did she find out you were sick?"

"Let me see." Ira tried to remember. "I must have mentioned it. See my plant here?" He pointed to the ivy on the table next to him. "She brought that for me when I had my appendix out. You must remember that time, Henry. You and Martha Helen both came to see me."

"She lives in Indiana now, this Sarah. Isn't that what you said?"

"Illinois."

"And you spoke with her." Mr. Parker's voice betrayed his concern.

"Yes, Henry."

"That is quite a ways."

"Yes, it is. She has quite a distance to come. That is why I wanted to know about the rain. Quite a trip in the rain. And remember, Henry, she is only seven."

4:30 P.M.

Dearest Phillip,

I have found that the quietest part of the day is from two to four in the afternoon. Already I hear some movement outside my door, people talking. I like the sound. Such a friendly group of people, although I will admit that I did find the commotion unsettling at first.

I am especially fond of Mrs. Bowdin, who visits me every day. I wrote you of the watch she gave me, and she frequently takes me to visit her other friends who are staying in the motel. She is a strange old woman, and some of her speech is quite surprising. But, Phillip, she is so kind to me. She regularly brings me fruit or some sweet (my waistline is beginning to show her generosity!). It breaks my heart to see her stumble so and curse her blindness. For all appearances, she has been forgotten by her family and friends. Thank God I have you.

Did you get in touch with Paul Wickerhurst? I was thinking the other day of that time in Dallas when the four of us

Kathleen stopped and listened. There was nothing for a moment and she started to resume her letter when she heard it again, a very light single tap against her door.

"Yes? Who is it?" Kathleen stood up and walked toward the door. "Yes?" She opened it a few inches. "Mrs. Bowdin!"

Azzie smiled faintly. "I didn't know whether you would be sleeping."

"No, I was writing to Phillip. Please come in."

Azzie looked down the hall blindly. "No, I think not. I haven't—I—" She gripped her cane. "I only came for a moment."

Kathleen stepped out into the hallway. "You're not ill? Are your eyes . . ."

"No, no." Azzie laughed shrilly. "I'm fit as a fiddle. The only thing is, Kathy, you see, I must get out of here. I must have my operation, I must get my sight back. You're the only one who understands that. You do understand," Azzie questioned, her cane nervously tapping the floor.

"Yes, of course. Of course I understand."

"I am not going to die here," Azzie continued quickly.

"You're the only one, the only one." Azzie shook her head. "They have stolen my letters. My letters to Mr. Roscoe. To everyone, every single one." Azzie's head was moving continuously now. "You must help me. Please. I am eighty-four, Kathy."

"I will help you." Kathleen put both her hands on Azzie's shoulders. "Please come inside."

"No," Azzie answered sharply. "Promise me that you will help me. Swear to it. You are my only friend. I thought Miss Zeagler . . . but she is useless."

"How can I help? I could write new letters."

"No. You must take me. Take me to Mr. Roscoe in Cambria. He will help me. My husband was one of the pillars of his organization; Mr. Roscoe told me so himself. He will take me to the Veterans Hospital. Please." Azzie found Kathleen's arm and squeezed it savagely. "Please."

"Yes," Kathleen answered without hesitating. "Phillip will be here any day now and we will take you to Cambria with us."

Azzie released her grip and smiled shakily. "Bless you, Kathy. I knew you would help me. I just knew it. Bless you."

"Are you going?" Kathleen asked as Azzie started off.

"Yes, dear. I don't have time to talk. I have to get some things in order. I'll see you tomorrow." Azzie turned around suddenly. "You wake me if he comes tonight."

"I don't think—"

Azzie waved her hand. "You wake me anytime he

comes. Day or night. I've slept all I want to sleep in this place."

Kathleen returned to her letter. She wrote:

Phillip, Mrs. Bowdin has just visited me and I told her we would take her to Cambria with us. To her friend, Mr. Roscoe. It is the least we can do. We are so lucky, you and I.

CHAPTER 15

Earl Brogdon was sitting up in his hospital bed watching "Concentration" when his wife came in, unannounced, wearing a scarlet dress with a high wide belt that herded a bit of gratuitous flesh about her ribs into a roll of red wool that rode like a protruding lip beneath her breasts. "Luisa!" He was surprised, elated.

"Hello, Earl." She had a dull voice, flattened by the sound of Texas.

"I didn't think you were coming."

"For heaven's sake, Earl." She pulled the visitor's chair as far away from her husband's bed as was possible in the tiny room. "You've just had surgery and I wanted to give it a little time to heal. Although"—she studied his bandaged ear—"it doesn't look so bad. I didn't know it would be wrapped up like that. You know how easily I get sick."

"Clay said you had a cold."

"That was months ago."

Earl touched his ear. "They're not through yet."

"Is that so?" She took two sticks of Doublemint from

her purse and rolled them into tight balls on her palm, one after the other. "Do they know?" Both sides of her mouth came down on fat wads.

"They won't tell me. Do you have any more gum?"

"No, this is my last. They would have told Clay if they did. Or me. I am your wife, after all."

Along with a complexity of other emotions, Earl felt a tremendous timidity toward his wife. When he asked, "Why did you wait so long to come and see me?" his voice was filled with it.

"I told you." She made her tone tediously patient. "I can't stand to see people cut up or wounded. It makes me throw up. As a matter of fact, Earl, I don't like hospitals at all, and I wouldn't be here if Clay hadn't insisted that you needed to see me. If somebody just saw you on the street, they wouldn't even have to know. You could tell them you got hit by a baseball or something." She popped her gum. "I don't understand what Clay was so up in the air about. You're not still hurting where you fell, are you?"

He shook his head. "Clay doesn't like me."

"What?" She stopped chewing. "Don't be silly, Earl. You ought to thank your lucky stars that you didn't break your hip. It wouldn't be hard to do at your age."

"What has Clay been telling you about me?"

"Do you want something, Earl? Would you like some magazines? We still get your old *Field and Stream* at the house. I could send some with Clay if you like." He started to answer. "Some candy?" she continued. "It is okay for you to have candy, isn't it?"

Earl watched two blocks turn on "Concentration" before he replied; it was not a match. "The other day"

—he spoke quietly—"I thought Clay had come to see me. Woke me up, but I was glad to see him. He made me get up." Earl shook his head incredulously. "He took me outside, to the top of the hill"—he gestured—"to tell me that I have cancer. Made me get up and go outside."

"You know, Earl"—Luisa Brogdon placed her gum in its foil wrapper with an elaborate motion of her tongue —"you shouldn't go around saying that people don't like you. You said that about me the whole time we were married." She caught the slip instantly. "Before you came here, I mean. Of course, we are still married." She stood up, gathering her purse and scarf, worrying the line of her dress. "It gives people ideas. Stupid thing to do."

"Clay has been telling you things!" Earl saw the look of disgust that flashed in her eyes and tried to vanquish it with a change in his tone. "I want to go home," he said. "I feel like going home, Luisa."

"You can't come home, pumpkin," she replied simply. "You can't ever come home again, not after your stroke. It would be too dangerous. I can't let you take that kind of chance."

"I am your husband," he replied.

"Yes, you are. And it is my responsibility to see that you are with people who can look after you." She was at the door. "I will send Clay tomorrow with some candy. I just bought some peanut brittle that—"

"Are you going out?"

"What are you talking about? Going out? With men?"

"You slut!"

She opened the door, triumphant. "Good-by, Earl."

"I'm sorry." He covered his eyes sadly. "I'm sorry."

159

"I know you are," she answered. "You just can't help yourself. I've learned that, believe me." She tugged at her tight belt. "On the way over here, I asked myself, 'How long will it be, Luisa Brogdon? How long will it be before your husband insults you, calls you names? What was it, Earl? Five minutes? Six? Let's be honest. You hate me. You hate me because I am not old and sick."

"No," he wailed. "I don't hate you."

"Well." She did not have to discuss it. "As we keep reminding ourselves, we are married, and I am glad that you are all right. Clay will be by to see you tomorrow."

"I didn't mean . . ." Earl began, but he could not think of exactly what he did and did not mean before she could close the door. Earl lay back, hating the throbbing in his ear, the sound of his voice.

Andrew Carlyle waited every evening at the end of the third ward for Azzie Bowdin to come teetering out of the room she shared with Jimi June and disappear around the turn in the corridor. She would be on her way to some mysterious visit or business, and Andrew would take his opportunity to be with Jimi June. As usual, he had waited in just this way every night of this week, but it was not until Thursday that Azzie decided to go out, and then only for a short time. She told Jimi June that she was going to the weekly singsong that was held in the community room.

Andrew turned the green-faced clock toward him. "What time did she say she would be back?"

"Nine. She wants to listen to the news."

"I came by here at noon and the news was on."

Jimi June shrugged. "She likes to hear it. She won't listen to anything else."

They were lying together on the single bed. His arm was loosely stretched across her stomach. He was sleepy; she was not and began to ask him again about the places he had been to, a list she had extracted countless times and forgotten just that many. "Colorado?" she asked. "My sister lives in Colorado."

"Yes." He let his eyes close. "I have been to Denver."

"I have never been there. I always wanted to go out and see her. California?" she asked.

"Yes." He yawned.

"Hawaii?"

"No. Jimi, we have been all through this."

She paid no attention. "Have you ever been to New York City?"

"Uh huh."

"With Angie?"

"Yeah."

"You have?" She edged closer to him.

"Yes." He rubbed his face. Eight-thirty.

"Every time?"

"She didn't like to stay home alone."

"Scared?" Jimi June demanded.

"I don't know." He tossed against her impatiently. "Why do you always ask about her?"

"I don't know," she answered him in the same way and sat up.

Andrew was irritated by her flippancy. "My Lord, are you jealous?" he demanded. "She is dead, Jimi. Has been for thirteen years."

She did not answer.

"I can't understand why you don't get off Angie," he persisted.

Jimi June swung her hips away from him and placed her bare feet on the floor. "I never knew anybody who was married. Except my sister, and I never see her."

"Is that it? Marriage?" He raised himself on one elbow. "Do you want to get married?"

She considered it abstractly. "I used to think about it."

"Do you?"

"To you?"

"To me!" he mocked nervously. "I mean, you don't have anybody else to marry. As long as you are so hopped up on the idea." He glanced at the clock; it was less than ten minutes to nine.

"Where would we go?"

"Maybe I could get us out of here. Or at least we could have a room together like Colloway and what's-her-name, his wife." Andrew gestured toward the empty bed. "You wouldn't have to live with her anymore."

Jimi June knelt on the floor beside the bed, searching for her cardboard box. "Would you like some Ritz? I took some from Sunday school last week."

"Jimi, answer me. Do you or don't you?"

She produced her shoe box. "My sister says . . ." she began quietly.

"I know." He ran his hand through his hair, pausing along the perimeter of his growing bald spot. "You know, Jimi, when you are young, a little pain in these things is a pleasure or it's nothing at all. Especially when it's not you that's feeling it. But I wouldn't hurt you." He stopped and retraced his words. "If you think it would hurt, then it's not important, although you wouldn't find many to agree with that. Okay?"

She nodded, biting into a stale Ritz cracker.

"Can you tell that my hair is falling out? Right here in back." He turned his head.

"Yes."

"Damn. Well, will you marry me?"

"Yes. Will you take me to Colorado?"

He chuckled and pulled her to him. "What's the matter? Are you scared to stay alone? Is that your problem?" He kissed her forehead lightly.

"Who's that? Who's that man talking?" Azzie cried from the doorway. It was four minutes after the hour.

Uncle Robert was sitting on the front porch watching two men repair a broken second-story window in the rear of the Baptist Church. "You see, Cranson, he is going to knock the rest of that window out before he does anything else. We never have seen a ladder that tall, have we? The tallest one I ever remember— Well, hello, Ira."

"Hello, Uncle Robert."

"How are you feeling, Ira?" Uncle Robert was delighted to see his friend after such a long time. "Henry said you had been under the weather. Oh, not there, please, Ira. Cranson is sitting there."

"Oh, excuse me." Ira quickly moved one chair down.

Uncle Robert whispered an explanation to the empty chair and then raised his head to address Ira. "This is only the second time Cranson has come outside with me all year. He didn't care for the summer, but it is getting cool enough for him now. Isn't that right, Cranson?"

Ira smiled faintly, thinking of something else.

"So tell me, Ira. How are you?"

"Fine."

"I'm glad to hear that. It's a terrible thing to be sick at this age. Everything hurts so much more. I stepped on something the other day"—he crossed his foot over his leg and held it up for Ira to see—"a little splinter or a needle, and by golly, my toe was sore in the morning. I had already taken off my shoes when I decided to go to the bathroom. That's how it happened. I used to go barefoot all the time when I was young and never picked up anything that gave me any trouble. People were always telling me I was going to get worms that way." He shook his head. "Never did. Neither did Cranson, and I never knew him to wear shoes before he reached his majority. Not even to church."

"Did you get the splinter out?" Ira asked.

"I hope so." Uncle Robert replaced his foot on the concrete. "Might have just pushed it in deeper; it's hard to tell. Sakes, it was painful. Ira." He pointed. "See those men over there? They are fixing the window of the church."

"I can see that." Ira nodded. "It's quite high up."

"It's some ladder," Uncle Robert agreed. "Now, I don't know a whole lot about ladders, but I'd bet that one belongs to a painter. That man up on top must have borrowed it from a painter friend of his. He was out here before, I'd say—oh—" Uncle Robert tilted his head far to the left. "What would you say, Cranson? An hour? You think that long?" He turned to wink at Ira. "As a compromise between two eyewitnesses, let's say an hour and a half. We didn't know what the devil he was up to, and Cranson here, being naturally suspicious, said it was to no good. But he went off after a while, and we thought that was the last of him. But pretty soon he was back with this other man and that ladder and they went to work."

"He must have been measuring the hole to see what size glass they would need," Ira speculated.

"From a baseball, I think. Happens all the time. The kids play right there in the parking lot. I just know someday I'm going to be lying in bed and one of those hard old balls is going to come flying through the window and land on top of me." He indicated the neighboring chair with his head and raised his eyebrows significantly. "I sleep on the window side. Cranson can't take the breeze. Imagine, Ira"—he stroked his chest—"a baseball sailing right through the window. You know how hard those things are."

"That would be a shock."

"A shock! Indeed."

Ira opened his legs slightly, handling his body with a recent sternness. The pods on the crape myrtle bush growing beyond the porch were shriveled and cold; the church maple was the color of sulfur. It was the time of year for catfishing with Sarah. He edged down a bit in his chair and tentatively breathed more deeply.

"Do you know how the buses run?" he asked Uncle Robert.

"The buses?" Uncle Robert crossed his ankles and leaned forward. "Well, I'll tell you something about that. My cousin had a time with the buses last spring."

"Oh? What was that?"

"He was coming to see me, I believe it was May, al-though"—Uncle Robert touched his hairless chin—"it might have been June already. He told the driver that he had to get off in Mount Virginia to transfer to a C. City bus because the one he was on didn't stop in India. But you know, that old bus driver let him off in Hampton; don't ask me why. Ira, that is his name, Ira. Same as you. Ira went to school several years in Jaksboro, but he speaks very plainly. I don't think that driver could have thought he said Hampton when Ira said plain as day Mount Virginia. Poor Ira sat around in Hampton, just a little gas station or a grocery store for a bus stop, I forgot which. Finally, after a whole afternoon and half the evening, he stopped a farmer to ask him what time the bus would be coming, and after a few minutes the farmer caught on that Ira was in the wrong place and offered to take him to Mount Virginia. But it was quite a thing, all in all."

Ira was concerned by the tale. "But what about children?" he asked anxiously. "I mean children traveling alone. Would they do that to a child?"

"Children." Uncle Robert shifted in his chair. "Children would be a different matter. The bus company has these little name tags"—he pointed to his lapel—"that they put on them, telling in black and white or red and white where they are going and who they belong to. Depending on the driver, he might even let them ride up front, give them some candy. I've seen it happen. That's the funny thing about drivers. They don't give a you-know-what about you or me, and I certainly wouldn't let Cranson ride alone, but children are a different matter altogether. Why do you want to know? You got a nephew or somebody coming to see you, Ira?"

"A little girl, a friend of mine," he answered and

pressed his small palms together. "I am still concerned about her riding the bus. She is only seven."

"Where is she coming from?"

"Illinois."

"That is a long way." Uncle Robert nodded appreciatively. "But I wouldn't worry. Cranson and I once went all the way to Kansas and back, and that was long before either of us was married. You know my sister passed away the other day?"

"No, I didn't. I am sorry to hear that."

"I guess you were sick when I got the news. A stroke; it was over just"—he snapped his fingers—"like that. I'm thankful she didn't suffer. Of course, she was a model Baptist, absolutely model. Knew every song in the book."

"I am very sorry to hear about your sister, Robert."

"Thank you, Ira." He glanced toward the church. "Look!" he cried in surprise. "They've picked up and gone. I didn't hear their truck starting up. You would think an old truck like that would make more noise."

"You can't tell that window was ever broken now."

"Sure can't. Say, where is Henry? I've been expecting him to come out all afternoon."

"A cousin of Martha Helen's came by to visit and brought him some chocolate cake. Quite a nice thing to do. Henry sure does love cake."

"Doc is working on his book. I'll be glad when he gets done with that. He hardly has time for a hand of gin anymore."

"Yes." Ira slyly watched his fingers begin to move on his pants leg. "I think I will go in, Robert. The doctor says I am supposed to have a nap along about now every day. I feel like I have been sleeping my life away lately."

"You do what he says," Uncle Robert instructed. "You have to take care of yourself, Ira. It pays at this age."

"I will do that, Uncle Robert," Ira said and stood up.

CHAPTER 16

"What the devil! What has happened?" Azzie slapped the back of a chair with her cane. "What's this doing here? I don't remember anything being right here in the doorway like this."

"I didn't hear you knock, Azalea," Ima Johnston replied pointedly, reluctantly looking up from her paperback novel.

"What in God's name happened to this place?" Azzie demanded again, ignoring the accusation.

"Just a bit of redecorating. I had the file cabinet moved into the closet, and so I—" She stopped. "What are you doing in here anyway?"

Azzie maneuvered herself around the offending chair and was seated. "I am here to issue a complaint."

Ima Johnston glanced down to page ninety-seven of *The Case of the Blonde Bombshell.* Perry Mason had just proposed to Della Street that they take a short trip to the scene of the crime. The time was ripe for romance: Perry was discouraged. He needed the support only Della could give him.

"I want to report an instance of vice."

"What?" Mrs. Johnston wrinkled her beak nose in puzzlement.

"Sex. You still call it that, don't you? Lascivious conduct." Azzie struck her cane on the uncarpeted floor. "S-e-x, sex. You would think she would be too old for that sort of thing. Lord knows, it's the last thing on *my* mind."

"Who's that?" Mrs. Johnston asked, closing her book. "Who are you talking about?"

"That crazy dodo I live with—who do you think? Sprawled out on that little bed like a couple—"

"With a man!"

"I couldn't see him at first. I'm so blind, I wouldn't see the Devil if he were standing in front of me waving his pitchfork and singing 'Dixie.'" She shook her head. "It's pitiful to be this way."

Ima Johnston began to be suspicious. "Are you sure there was a man at all?"

"I blocked the scoundrel's way!" Azzie retorted indignantly. "He was big, I mean to tell you, but I stood my ground. 'Who are you?' I shouted. 'Identify yourself.'"

"I'll bet I know," Mrs. Johnston offered, animated. "Emit Street. I never have trusted that man."

Azzie leaned back in her chair and said nothing.

"Well, am I right?"

"You won't believe it." She made her voice quiet and doleful. "I could hardly believe it myself. Of all people, Andrew Carlyle."

"Mr. Carlyle!"

"I couldn't believe it myself."

Ima Johnston chuckled harshly. "I guess men never

change. After they get away from their mothers, they never change until the day they die. I had an uncle just like that. We finally had to ask him to quit coming to the family reunions; it was that bad."

"I want someone new."

"I will certainly have a word with that Mr. Carlyle."

Azzie raised her nose. "You've got to find me somebody new. You've been keeping me in the same room with a sex fiend, a small room at that, and I demand a change. Besides," she added in a victorious tone, "it is only for a few days."

"A few days?" Ima Johnston dropped her head and shook it back and forth in a loose arch. "No siree. If I move you again, Azalea, you are going to have to stay put. I think you have been with just about all the women here. Have to start a second round, I guess. Say, did you hear that joke about Alaska? I don't know what made me think of this"—she began to laugh as an undertone—"but you know they say it is bigger than Texas. You know what we say back at them? Wait till the ice melts!" She rolled her eyes and let her laugh go wild.

"I want to move or I want somebody new."

"Well." Mrs. Johnston rolled her eyes and tried to forget about her joke. "I don't know who else to try. Except Kathleen Storrs in the single. Maybe she would trade with Jimi June." She rubbed a tear into her nose and half-restrained a low chuckle. "Wait till the ice melts."

"Phillip is going to stay with her for a few days and so she will need her room. But inside of a week we shall both be gone—good riddance to this place. But until then I want Jimi June out of my room. How about Fronie

MacDermott? She stays out of the room most of the time anyway, playing cards and gambling. I could take that for a few days."

"What do you mean, you'll be gone? Gone where? And what's this about some man moving in with Mrs. Storrs? It sounds like more sexy stuff to me."

Azzie tightened a green kerchief she had tied around her loose bun; the flowered ends fell at odd angles onto her round forehead, giving her the appearance of a haphazardly dressed baby doll. "Her husband, Phillip. We expect him today or tomorrow, and after he rests for a while, he will be taking both Kathleen and me back to Cambria." She smiled in spite of herself. "I have a very close friend in Cambria, Mr. Roscoe, a friend and admirer of my late husband's. He is going to take me to the Veterans Hospital for my operation. Mr. Roscoe has always—"

"Mrs. Storrs has no husband."

"Don't be silly." Azzie drew her eyebrows together quickly. "Her name is Mrs., isn't it? Phillip has just been away on some sort of trip. We expect him back any—"

"I am just—"

"Quit interrupting me!" Azzie demanded. "We expect him back any day now."

"You must have your numbers or people or years mixed up, Azalea. Are you sure you mean"—she turned to consult a typed list of room assignments she had taped on the wall close to her desk—"Kathleen Storrs in 25B?"

"Do you think I would go off with a stranger?" Azzie huffed and pulled herself erect. "Of course I mean Kathy Storrs. My dearest friend."

"If I had a hundred dollars"—Mrs. Johnston walked

toward a small closet near the door to her office—"I would bet you the whole thing that she has no husband." She opened a small file box and after some hunting removed a sheet of white paper.

Azzie was staring fiercely in the direction of her voice. "What are you doing?" Azzie demanded.

"This is the only thing we have on Mrs. Storrs." Ima Johnston waved the sheet. "It makes it so difficult to deal with the state when there is no more information than this, especially when you have to ask for some kind of assistance for the person." She read, " 'Born eighteen eighty-one. Husband Phillip, died nineteen forty-eight. No children. No medical insurance.' I thought that was the case."

"It's not true."

"That's sure as the world what this paper says. She has a cousin around somewhere. He brought her here, but he hasn't been around since. I'll have one of the aides ask her today about switching with Jimi June."

Azzie leaned forward dully, holding the bottom of her chair with both hands, still staring at the undefined world in front of her. "You know," she said finally,"I got a letter from Peggy the other day, a nice long letter."

"I don't remember seeing any letter from Peggy."

"Oh, yes, I did," Azzie answered slowly. "I remember. I remember every word."

Kathleen straightened the blanket covering her bed for the fourth time in the hour, which she noticed, checking her watch, was almost over. Occupants of the neighboring rooms would soon be going to bed. Mrs. Boswell across the hall had told Kathleen that she had never gone to bed after nine-thirty a night in her life, a fact that seemed curious to Kathleen, who was accustomed to staying up until early morning with Phillip. But no matter, she thought, and picked up a paper cup filled with hard candies. There was still time left in the evening to visit Mrs. Bowdin.

Or perhaps not, Kathleen reconsidered when she reached 7C. The door was open. The friend who shared the room was not in sight and Azzie Bowdin appeared to be sleeping. Her head was off the pillow and her mouth was open and wet. "Mrs. Bowdin?"

Azzie shook her head, jarring her puffy eyes open.

"Mrs. Bowdin? Are you sleeping?"

"Yes? Who is it?"

Kathleen hesitated, feeling shy. "I am sorry I bothered you. Please."

"Please what. Who is it? Come here where I can see you."

"It is me—Kathleen," she answered without moving.

Azzie pursed her lips in disgust. "Kathleen."

"You have not been by to see me for the past week, and I was worried about you. I brought you some candy —last Thursday was a holiday, you know, and I found this on my tray." Kathleen offered the green-and-orange-striped paper cup. "I know how you like sweet things, and there seemed to be all kinds of things in here. Some lemon drops and some hard cherry candies."

"I don't want any."

"Are you ill? I hope you haven't caught a cold. The weather has turned so suddenly. I had been using just a thin sweater, but today I unpacked this heavy wrap. I had thought that Phillip would certainly be here before I would need this."

Azzie propelled herself onto her side and raised up on one elbow; her eyes stopped on the blurred form a few feet away from her. "Filthy liar."

"What?" Kathleen caught her breath shortly. "What did you say?"

"Filthy liar! If Phillip Storrs comes here, it will be as a ghost."

"You are—" Kathleen looked away, horrified. "He should be here tomorrow. We will take you back to Cambria, to your friend." Kathleen clasped her hands together and released them. "You are confused."

"And you are about eight years too late. 'Died,' " Azzie quoted, " 'nineteen forty-eight.' Get out of here."

"I don't lie," Kathleen pleaded. "Please don't say things like that to me. They are so hard to take back."

Azzie turned her eyes toward the hazy expanse of mustard wall and did not reply.

Kathleen was thinking of the man who had lived in the room before her, the sick man. Her fingers raced along the bleached green wallpaper, the only room in the entire motel with wallpaper, so the woman had said. What was her name? Something common on a tall woman. And what of the man? He must have died; Kathleen could remember nothing else being said, just that he had fallen ill at the same time the room was being remade into a small study, or for some other function that would explain the wallpaper. It had indeed been offered only by way of explanation, and the large woman had rushed on in a grating voice to discuss meals and laundry service. Nothing more was said of the sick man, but Kathleen remembered because she slept in the bed he had once slept in, and perhaps he had stared at the heavy maroon drapes and had similar thoughts.

Kathleen pushed herself away from the wall. If she had given Phillip children, everything would have been different. He never would have gone away if there were a little girl involved. Or a son. A son is what he . . .

He said it did not matter and it did not matter. He would be coming for her any day now; he had told her so and he would not lie. Kathleen went to her bed. He would not write to her either. She pulled a thread from her black skirt. She could not remember the precise distance between his letters, but it seemed longer than a few days or a week. Her watch said two thirty-two. Kathleen stretched out on her bed, her head wrinkling the corner of the evening's letter.

She sat by the window and shuffled her three last sheets of white paper. Two were already filled with many narrow lines, crossed through with a quick hand many times until the ideas themselves were abandoned. Kathleen framed the last sheet with a nervous hand and tried to be careful of her writing.

"Dearest Phillip," she began. "I have been waiting to hear from you. I want to know where you are. Please cable or telephone the motel. I have to know at least where you are. There is nothing wrong or urgent, but not being accustomed to having to demand"

The grammar was incorrect and she hurried on.

"I am unhappy here. Please come and take me to another motel. Drive me back to the Alamo, even if you cannot stay with me. I don't have the money for such an emergency, and the people here dislike me. I don't eat."

Kathleen paused and touched her pen to her lips. She raised the paper higher up on her knee and began once more, this time near the center of the page.

My darling Phillip,

The doctor called this afternoon—he is completely sure! I am so happy and relieved. We have waited so long for this—I already feel differently. But don't let such statements start you worrying. I am doing everything that he tells me, and tonight I asked for a double portion of vegetables.

Phillip, it is time I was at home now. I am sure you understand my asking you this. I love you, darling—I know you must be as happy as I. I look for you.

Kathleen

Her wrist was tired from so much writing. She folded the letter clumsily and added it to the others in her top drawer, but she had no envelope and no string for binding. She had been without these things for some time, although she did not remember the exact day she had run out. It might be possible to count the loose letters and remember, but instead Kathleen returned to the window and opened the drapes.

It was the uncertain time mingling the last hour which could be linked to the night with the charcoal nuances of morning. Her watch read five-fifteen. Kathleen stripped herself of a Serendipity dress and the stockings she had been wearing for not quite a full day and put on a faded shift of denim and red cotton with deep pockets and a tear on the short sleeve. She wrapped the red tie belt twice around her waist and made a small, neat bow that gave her pleasure. She had not worn her cleaning dress for many months.

She wrote on the back of a brown sack that had previously lined her wastebasket.

Dear Phillip,

Darling. Our home is in such a state! You know what a squirrel I am, saving everything that I find or am given, so although I have tried to keep the house clean, you can imagine that in your absence the closets have grown quite cluttered. I don't mean to complain—I think of your coming home every time I pull out another long-ago discarded pair of shoes or a picture painted by some friend of a third cousin and given to us some Christmas past. I may not look quite the same to you, Phillip. It occurred to me the other day that there seems to be something quite different about my hair. And my hands. I do love this house. Everything will be clean and in order for your return.

She took her green bag from the closet and opened it: a shawl, two cardigan sweaters, one of blue and one of a yellow-and-pink harlequin design, a rust skirt, and a pair of wool stockings. Kathleen buttoned the sweaters, refolded them, and added the few clothes from her drawers, tucking her underwear along the edges and the bottom of her suitcase as was her custom. Her mirror and book of Teasdale she placed together between the folds of her skirt.

Phillip's suitcase was much heavier, filled with thick academic papers bound on steel rods, journals, and a vast number of newspaper clippings that Kathleen had saved over the years. She slid the suitcase along the floor to the bed and kicked it over with her feet. There was a tarnished gold lock on the front between two side buckles, and Kathleen went to her purse to get the tiny triple-toothed key which would open it.

CHAPTER 17

"Do you know how old I am, Cranson? I always thought you knew right along, year to year, but it occurs to me that perhaps I never told you. Old enough." Uncle Robert laughed. "That's what they always say, isn't it? Or too old. 'When I grow too old to dream,' " he sang softly, not to wake the man sleeping in the other bed. "Remember that song, Cranson? I do. I remember all kinds of things. Almost everything, I think. I didn't used to, but it comes back to me more and more. I remember Edna. Thin, but she had a—" He stopped short. "Oh, no." Uncle Robert shook his head emphatically. "Imagine me talking to you like this, a gossip like you. No, sir, Cranson. You're tricky, but not another peep out of me on this subject.

"Henry's all worked up about the Communists, did I tell you? I had an uncle that was ahead of everybody on this. He's dead now, you wouldn't remember him, but around nineteen twenty or twenty-one, he was already aware that there was something fishy in Siberia. I wish he had lived. He would be pretty old by now, over a hundred, but he sure would take Henry for all he was worth.

'Worried, are you!' he'd shout. 'You so-and-so softie! Why, if you was really worried you'd have your gun at your side at all times. Where is it?' And then he'd open up his coat and, sure thing, he'd have his own gun strapped to his trousers. He'd be fun to have here, and you would like him, Cranson. He knew a lot of your jokes."

"Look over there." Henry Parker pointed with obvious glee. "Son of a gun. Muriel Tyler has gone and dyed her hair red. She was always talking about it, and now she's gone and done it. My God. Red, of all colors, with her complexion. I wonder what Dorothy thinks about that. She told me once that Muriel was a little on the wild side."

"This meal is cold," Ira complained.

"You would think Muriel would grow out of it. She must be in her mid-fifties by now." Mr. Parker turned to Ira and smiled. "I like Sundays, having people come by like this, eat lunch with us. Reminds me a little bit of Sundays at the Crystal."

"I don't know how they expect us to live on this food." Ira stuck a prong of his fork through a portion of boiled chicken.

"That is what I have been saying exactly."

"It is not good for me while I am ill."

"I thought you were all right now." Mr. Parker was distracted by the activity of Elizabeth Colloway, who had just upset a bowl of oatmeal. Marsh Colloway was earnestly trying to cover the soggy tablecloth with a single napkin while his wife licked at a film of milk and oats oozing from her mouth.

"It comes and goes."

Henry Parker glanced back at Ira. "You seemed fine a couple of weeks ago."

"I was sleeping all the time," Ira corrected him. "All that medicine they were giving me. I don't want to sleep straight through Sarah's visit." He looked down; his hands were shaking slightly but he was uninterested and left them on the table.

"When is she coming?"

"I think anytime now."

Mr. Parker buttered a dinner roll generously. "You've been saying that since Halloween. It's past Thanksgiving now." He studied the table. "You don't see any jam anywhere, do you?"

"She told me she was coming immediately."

"That was when you talked with her?"

Ira nodded, taking a sip of lemonade, a Sunday special. "The lima beans were the only good part of the meal. I suppose they froze them from this summer."

"When was that?"

"What?" Ira pulled his lips between his fingers and released them. "This summer?"

"When was it that you talked with this little girl?"

"Sarah, Henry. She has a name."

Mr. Parker leaned forward. "Sarah." He made four syllables of it.

Ira shrugged. "I'd have to think about it to tell you exactly. A few days ago."

"Then you have talked with her again. You must have quite a phone bill. All the way to Indiana."

"Illinois."

"Illinois, dammit. I can't keep that straight." He took

a spoonful of peach ice cream. "I don't think I ever knew anybody from that state. I used to deal with people from all over in the bank, but never Illinois. That I recall anyways."

"You know what she said, Henry?" Ira looked away from his friend shyly. "I will never forget."

"Why? What did she say? This ice cream is good, Ira. You should try yours."

" 'I love you,' that's what she said, Henry. I will never forget the look on that child's face. 'You are my best friend,' she said, and 'I love you.' " Ira carefully touched the fingers of his left hand to those of his right. "We even took one of those oaths that kids have. 'I love you.' Do you understand, Henry?"

Mr. Parker was silent for a few minutes. He tipped his glass of lemonade and let several drops run onto his fingers. "And you think she will be coming any day, do you, Ira?"

Ira's fingers waved against each other silently. "Yes, that is what she said. She will have to ride the bus, all the way. I'd think that is at least seven hundred miles, wouldn't you, Henry?" He chuckled abruptly and ran one hand across his eyes. "Sarah won't mind. I believe she would walk that seven hundred miles, just to see her old friend Mr. Snow."

"Do you want my peas? I'm not going to eat them." Mr. Parker pushed his plate across to Ira. "How long have you known this Sarah?"

"Oh." Ira considered it. "It has been a good while. I'd say almost four years."

"Before you came here?"

"Yes, that's right."

"And you have been here about fourteen months."
Mr. Parker frowned. "How old did you say this little girl
is?"

"Seven." Ira tried to press his hands flat against the
table. "I have told you how many times before? Seven."

"Two," Henry Parker said softly, doing the arithmetic.
"Did you tell the front desk to expect this child?"

"No, but that is a good idea. Thank you, Henry."

"They can be sticky when the visitor is not one of the
family. Not always, but I have heard stories." Mr. Parker
coughed dryly and wiped his lips with a cotton napkin.
"It would be a shame for her to come all that way and
then not be let in to see you."

Ira forgot his hands, which were beginning to tremble
more noticeably, and moved toward Henry Parker. "You
don't think that has happened, do you? You don't think
that she came, came when she said she would, and they
sent her away?"

Mr. Parker shook his head. "You would have heard
something. News like that gets around."

"God, I hope not." Ira raised his hands toward his
face.

"What is this?" Mr. Parker caught several of the quivering fingers in a rough grasp. "What does this mean,
Ira? Are you in pain?"

"No, not at all. It is nothing."

"I thought the pills were supposed to help this."
Ira hesitated.

"Maybe the doctor should increase your dosage. Ask
him about it the next time he comes around."

"I want to be awake when Sarah comes."

"What! Don't be a fool, Ira. They were helping you.

Look at your hands." Henry Parker turned Ira's hand over in his palm and pried the fingers open. "Look at that, Ira. Are your feet going, too? Remember the night of the party, Ira. You know what can happen."

Ira reclaimed his fist. "Don't talk to me about it, Henry. I have to see her. Don't you understand? Can't you understand that, Henry? After she comes, I'll take all the pills you want." He met his friend's look of concern but did not soften. "I will."

It was Thursday afternoon, three days after Andrew had talked with Ima Johnston about marrying Jimi June. He stood in front of the brown easy chair in the community room.

"I need to talk to you."

She kept her eyes coldly fixed on the television screen.

"Come on, Jimi, this is important."

"I'm watching my program."

"Hello, Andrew," Miss Zeagler whispered shyly from the couch. Jimi June quickly shifted the gaze of her tiny round animal eyes.

"I'm asking you to come with me, Jimi. Just for a few minutes during the commercial. I have something to tell you."

"You're in my way!" Dorothy Tyler shouted at him.

"I thought you were sick," Jimi June replied. "I haven't seen you in a week."

"It's been four days, but I can explain all of that. Come outside where I can talk to you, Jimi." He took her limp hand in his.

"Get out if you're not going to watch," Mrs. Tyler commanded.

"All right, dammit. I tried."

"Carlyle." It was issued as an invitation of sorts, but Andrew was already past the doorway.

Dorothy Tyler and Jimi June had been living together for one hundred and forty-nine hours, and the only words they had spoken had passed between them when Jimi June first walked into the room carrying her single orange leather suitcase.

"You don't play cards," Dorothy Tyler announced flatly.

"No," Jimi June agreed.

"Neither did any of my husbands," Mrs. Tyler returned in an ominous tone.

This evening Dorothy Tyler was playing a crowded game of solitaire on a short rollaway table while Jimi June changed her clothes. Jimi June had two dresses, one not better than the other; she simply put on the one she had not yet worn that day. It was long, below her shin, and broadly striped in mauve and lime. Jimi June took a cautionary look over her shoulder and secretly splashed herself with her roommate's toilet water, Mon Amour.

Jimi June left her new room and walked to the front of ward A, stopping in front of the first door on the left. She started to knock, but she decided it was beside the point and walked in. Woodrow Barker was asleep in his bed. Andrew was sitting on the edge of his, swinging his feet in large circles, his shoes scuffing the floor with a dog-whistle sound.

"I came to see if you were sick." She touched the tiny blue cotton bow she had pinned to the downy gray lock growing in above her forehead.

"I never felt better."

"Well." She turned her face away from his and took a deep breath, imagining the lines of her breasts expanding. "I figured you had just changed your mind about getting married and I came to tell you that I don't care one bit. You are free to go."

He slid off his bed easily, no longer angry, and stood up. "You idiot. That's not it at all. Things can't be exactly like you wanted them, that's all I had to say."

"What?" She sat in the chair opposite him, her hands clasped together and held to her chest.

He decided not to tell her the truth. "A relocated mental case," Ima Johnston had called her. "We can't have the big party like you wanted," he began cautiously. "In fact, we can't let anybody know we are getting married."

"Why not?" She regarded him suspiciously. "Don't you believe in Jesus?"

"That has nothing to do with it." Andrew rubbed his head, his fingers pausing over his growing baldness. "I am too old."

Her look of incredulity spurred him on. "Now, don't look like that; I feel bad enough already. How old are you?"

"Sixty-six."

"Well, see, that's the rub. I'm seventy-two, and the State of Texas won't issue a license to anybody over seventy."

"Mr. Colloway is older than that."

"That doesn't count. Marsh Colloway's been married since before he knew what to do with what. But he could never change women now and get somebody new. He's way over the line. There's only one way to do it after you get to be as old as Marsh and I."

"How is that?"

"There's no use me telling you because you wouldn't be willing to do it. I think we'd better just call the whole thing off."

"Yes, I would."

"I don't think so."

Jimi June flashed her small eyes. "I would do it."

"We couldn't tell anybody," he repeated, "because if it got out, they might lock me up or something. They could look at my driver's license and see that I am over seventy."

"The preacher would know."

"Well, I'll tell you about that. People get married all kinds of ways, and not all of them need preachers. I've read about couples doing it in the middle of some desert, or on the top of the Empire State Building. It doesn't matter as long as you repeat certain words."

"What words?"

Andrew paused while Woodrow Barker turned himself onto his stomach, his heavy intake of breath lapsing momentarily. "Just something about how you're not going to run off, leaving a bad mortgage, that sort of thing. You're not planning on running off, are you?"

"They won't even let me go to town," Jimi June answered.

"That's what I mean." Andrew slapped his knee, encouraged by her slight smile. "We don't need a preacher and a bunch of witnesses for a simple thing like this. I say there's no reason not to go ahead and do it now. What do you say? . . .

"I have a wedding present for you," he coaxed when she did not reply immediately. He went to his closet and returned with a green-and-purple sack from Robinson's Drugs. "This is for you." Andrew felt around in the bottom of the sack until he found the wide gold band.

Jimi June accepted it eagerly, holding it in her open palm. "What's all this junk it's got on it? My sister's doesn't have anything like that on hers."

"Junk? What junk?" He leaned near her to examine the ring. "That's not junk, those are decorations. Geometric decorations. That's so you can tell yours apart from every other woman's. It's special," he added defensively.

"Thank you, Carlyle."

"Yeah." He nodded. "You can wear it right now, but take it off when you leave."

"I think about you a lot, Carlyle."

"Well, you can start thinking about me less and less because we're all tied up now." He brushed her cheek with his lips lightly. "I don't suppose we'll be able to get a room together right off, so I got you something to keep you company." He reached into the drugstore sack again and pulled out a fat orange-and-black stuffed tiger with a starched green bow tied about its neck. "It's not gray, but it sure as hell is a cat."

"Doris!" Jimi June took the toy to her chest. "That's what I'm going to call her. I always wished I was named Doris." She poked its emerald eyes playfully. "This is a fine wedding, Carlyle."

He acknowledged her pleasure with obvious relief and kissed her cheek again, this time more seriously. "What's done is done. Just be sure you keep that ring hidden."

"Sure thing." Her fingers followed the stiff curled tail of her cat.

At one-thirty on Friday afternoon, Henrietta Newman reported to Ima Johnston that the seventh tray had been taken from Mrs. Storrs's room untouched. Mrs. Newman had mentioned in passing that the woman was growing thin; nevertheless, Mrs. Johnston was stunned when she entered room 25B, armed with a candy bar and a determination to see what all the nonsense was about.

It had been six months since she had admitted Kathleen Storrs to Twilight Days. She remembered her as a slender woman, but not gaunt. The woman in the bed had eyes rimmed and dark. Tiny veins and bones showed in her hands, arranged on either side of her narrow hips. Her breath was slight; her breast rose not at all. Her hair was tied behind her neck with a brown, yellow, and orange printed scarf, and she wore a denim dress.

"Hello there, Mrs. Storrs." Mrs. Johnston greeted her cheerfully. "Do you remember me?"

Kathleen opened her eyes. Black pupils seemed to stretch around the curve of her eyes, deep and enormous like the eyes of a young French girl influenced by belladonna.

"You talked to me on your first day here—Mrs. Johnston, Ima Johnston. It's been a little while ago."

She sat down on the bed. Kathleen's eyes did not follow her. "This business of not eating can't go on, Mrs. Storrs. Are you ill?" She unwrapped the Mars candy bar. "I know that sometimes a person just doesn't feel like boiled meat and potatoes, so I brought you a little treat." She pressed the opened end of the candy to Kathleen's lips. "I'd eat it myself if I weren't ten pounds overweight. Just a little bite." She insisted with her hand, smearing the chocolate. "Give you some energy."

Kathleen closed her eyes.

"Try, Mrs. Storrs. You've got to eat something before you fade into these bedsprings."

Kathleen did not respond. Mrs. Johnston bit off the unwrapped part of the bar and put the rest into her pocket. She tried the seduction several more times during the day, with some fruit and a piece of cake. Once she noticed the section of newspaper on the floor beside Kathleen's bed, but she did not bother to pick it up, put out as she was by Kathleen's continued obstinacy. It was an article with a small accompanying photograph that Kathleen had been saving since April of 1948.

CHAPTER 18

Christmas decorations always went up on the Monday morning marking the second week in December, and on that day Vidy Phillips presented herself in the community room, dangling a red bulb she had appropriated from last year's Christmas tree. "I am here to decorate," she announced to the two women who were stringing ribbons of plastic holly across the ceiling.

Bess Turner exchanged looks with Henrietta Newman, who was standing midway up a short stepladder. "The tree isn't here yet, Vidy."

"No, Vidy," Mrs. Newman echoed. "It won't be here for hours. Why don't you go back to your room and we'll call you as soon as it gets here."

Vidy smiled amiably and worked her tongue. "I don't mind waiting," she declared and took a seat on the couch, carefully cradling her ornament. "I think he does a good job, don't you?"

"Who's that, Vidy?"

"Yeah," Vidy agreed. "We told him that. He came to see us once, you know. It was hot, a hundred degrees, and he brought his little spot dog with him. He wanted to know how was he doing, and we all said he was doing fine." On the table next to the couch was a paper reindeer with a balloon stomach, which Vidy poked merrily. "Yes siree."

Henrietta Newman attached the end of a string of light-green holly to the ceiling with a thumbtack. "What do you want for Christmas, Vidy?"

"I think some pudding would be good, don't you?" Vidy licked her lips. "Well, hello, Becky."

"Hello yourself," Becky Springer croaked from the doorway. "What's doing in here?"

"We're getting ready for Santy Claus," Vidy answered.

"Santa Claus!" Becky looked at the two aides with sharp disapproval. "Why don't one of you tell her?"

"Come on in," Vidy beckoned. "He's bringing the tree before too long."

"Nah. I've got things to do." Becky reached into the pocket of her gingham apron and pulled out an old Christmas card reading, "Best Wishes for a Joyous Season, Christmas 1949, from Bobbie, Jack, and the Kids." On the back, with the help of Fronie MacDermott's steady hand, Becky had transcribed her Last Will and Testament. In the first of nine lines she remembered Fronie for her trouble and bequeathed to her a red slip and padded brassiere that had been given to her several birthdays ago by a long-time neighbor. "You need it more than I do," Becky had declared, surveying Fronie's thin figure. To Vidy she left her mail-order flower catalogue and whatever Coke money she would have left at the front desk at the time of her death. To her cousin, the Bobbie of the Christmas card, she willed two bird pictures that had hung in her living room for years. "I don't care what happens to the rest of it," the will concluded. "Nobody will look after my plants anyway, so I don't care what happens to them as long as nobody starts digging them up and taking them home." It was signed Rebecca Adelade Springer.

Becky maneuvered her slow big body through the doorway and waddled a few steps forward toward Bess Turner. "Here, this is for you."

"My, what a pretty card."

"I think so," Becky replied.

"Well, thank you. Thank you very much." Mrs. Turner smiled at Becky. "This is the first card anyone has given to me this season. Of course, I haven't sent mine out yet, and that always makes a difference."

"It isn't for you," Becky explained disdainfully. "This is my will."

"Your will?" Mrs. Turner looked at the demure Mary holding a fat sleeping child against a purple twilight.

"On the back. Turn it over to the back."

"Oh, I see." She nodded, finding the tiny, even lines of handwriting. "To Bonnie? Is that what it says?"

"It's none of your business what it says!" Becky admonished. "I want you to lock it away. Put it in a safe until my time comes."

Henrietta Newman was winding red thread around a wire frame to make a poinsettia. "I don't think it's legal done like that, without a lawyer to sign it."

Becky ignored her and leaned close to Bess Turner, her scrapy voice deepening. "Don't you let anything happen to that card."

"I'll be back with you before they bring the cups

around, don't you worry," Vidy called to Becky as she left the room.

It was after two when the tree finally arrived, a fine full tree, and by the time it was upright and secure in its stand, four more decorators had joined the proceedings: Jimi June, Jason Hadley, Fronie MacDermott, and Uncle Robert, who insisted on hanging only blue bulbs and in close proximity. Jimi June, who far preferred to drape the tinsel, was instructed to follow behind him, breaking up his clusters with an assortment of different colors. "I don't even like blue," she muttered and stepped on the back of Uncle Robert's heel.

Ira pulled the blanket close around himself and sat on his hands when he heard his door opening, but both his legs were trembling and the cover did not conceal them.

"How are you feeling, Mr. Snow?" Bess Turner asked, glancing at the movement near the bottom of his bed.

"Fine, thank you." He tried an easy gesture with his head.

"That is good to hear." She placed his midafternoon orange juice and pill on the table beside him. "Christmas is a terrible time to be sick. I remember once when I was a little girl, I got the flu right about this time, and I thought at the time what a shame it was to be lying in bed, not able to enjoy everything. Especially now, with Christmas only two weeks away." She pulled the curtains open and began to dust the sill with the corner of her slip. "Think of that! I have so much shopping left to do. And you have a birthday coming up."

"Is it your birthday already, Ira?"

"I hadn't remembered," Ira replied to Mr. Parker, slipping the pill into his ear.

Mrs. Turner turned around. "Why, of course it is. I know you are scheduled for the birthday party on Friday, so it must be sometime this month. What day were you born on?"

Ira laughed slowly. "To tell you the truth, I don't think I remember anymore." He turned his head very carefully and opened the drawer of the end table he shared with Mr. Parker. "Have you seen my blue book, Henry?"

"What book is that?"

The movement of his hands attracted Ira's attention: one finger knocked against the table and he withdrew his hand. "Some book Uncle Robert gave me. A novel. It was a birthday present, and it had the date written in the front. Do you see it, Henry?"

Mr. Parker rolled onto his side. "A blue book? What is all this stuff in here anyway, Ira?" He displayed a folded paper cup and a pencil with the lead broken off. "Oh, here it is." He opened the cover. "To Ira, on the occasion of his birthday, December nineteenth, nineteen fifty-four."

"Yes." Ira nodded. "I was seventy-five that year."

"December nineteenth—that is a week from Sunday." Mrs. Turner was near his bed. "But the party will be on Friday, the second Friday of the month, just as always. Do you think you will be feeling up to it?"

Sarah was waiting for his birthday. This was the reason she had not come. "Oh, yes." Ira smiled. "I am certain that I will."

"I hate those damn parties."

Ira closed his eyes. His mood was lightened. "You

always go when it is your birthday, Henry," he teased. "You always go in May."

"Humph."

Bess Turner paused on her way out the door, frowning at the movement beneath Ira's gray blanket. "You are taking your pills, aren't you, Mr. Snow? You did take the one I just gave you?"

"Of course." He heard Henry Parker move in his bed.

"That's good." She smiled at him quickly. "I want you to be feeling well for your party."

"Will there be cake?" he asked.

"Yes. Chocolate this month, I think."

"Sarah will like that," Ira replied, too softly for anyone to hear.

Earl Brogdon moved and a flurry of thin wood shavings fell from his lap to the floor. He absently touched the flat surface that had been his ear and went on with his work. He was making candle holders for Luisa's Christmas present. In the bed across from him, Max Churcher was in his fourth hour of sleep. He was shirtless, his grayish, picked back exposed, but Earl did not look in his direction. The slab of walnut was beginning to take form: Christmas was exactly two weeks away.

Azzie was waiting in the hallway when Bess Turner passed by. "Hello!" Azzie cried out, taking a few steps toward the white uniform.

"Hello, Azalea."

"I've been waiting for you." Azzie smiled. "Who are you anyway? Mrs. Newferry?"

"No; Mrs. Turner."

"Oh, yes." Azzie's smile widened. "I know you. I do indeed."

"I'm in a bit of a hurry, you know."

"Yes, well." Azzie's cane hit the aide's leg softly. "I wanted to talk to you. I've been waiting here all this time just for the chance. It is hard for me to stand up like this; I'm old. Eighty-four."

"What did you want to ask me about?" Mrs. Turner glanced at her watch. It was ten minutes to four, twenty minutes after the time for Kathleen Storrs's afternoon injection.

"About this woman they've put me with. She's crazy. She talks to herself, gibberish. Do wah wah wa." Azzie leaned close to Mrs. Turner and breathed on her neck. "The first time she got going, I thought there was a baby in the room. The way I can't see, for all I knew somebody had dropped one right there on my doorstep. That's just what she sounds like. But no, ma'am. I searched every inch of that room and finally I got over to where she was. I got real close. It's her, all right."

"I'm sorry, but there's nothing I can do about El-berta."

"You expect me to just live with that? I just got rid of one lunatic; no telling what kind of damage she did to me."

"Can we talk about this later? I really do have to go. I'm already a half hour late for Mrs. Storrs's feeding."

"Mrs. Storrs?" Azzie repeated sharply. "What does she need to be fed for? It's not time for dinner."

"No, it's not a meal like that; it's a shot."

"What kind of a shot?"

"My, aren't you nosy? She hasn't been eating, not a

thing, and she needs this to keep her going. Now go on back to your room, you hear?"

Azzie nodded, but she did not move. It was the first she had heard about Kathleen.

CHAPTER 19

The room smelled, Azzie noted with surprise. She had never considered Kathleen an unclean person, but there was no denying that her room held a damp odor like an unused cellar where perhaps some flowering plant had been set in water and left too long, leaving its dark green stain on the sides of the pot and where the leaves touched the wall. Azzie shook her head, trying to dissipate the smell. "Kathleen." She encountered a familiar object, the chair in which she had sat during her evening visits to this room; but it was out of place, moved much closer to the bed. Azzie carefully made her way around to the front of it and sat down.

"Kathleen. What is it? You are not going to speak to me? I have come all this way, after how you treated me. Lied to me. I hate liars. I wish you would answer me." She worked her hands nervously. "Kathleen?"

Azzie pushed herself from the chair. "Are you ill?" she yelled. "What is wrong with you? Are you sick? Is it something you ate, something they gave you here?"

Kathleen did not answer. Azzie let herself back into the chair, her eyes fixed on the expanse of white and dark ahead of her. After a time her gaze became dumb and she let her head go to her chest in a heavy nap.

She was awakened by a sound from outside the room. "What?" She turned her head sleepily. "Oh, Kathleen." She brushed her eyes. "I fell asleep." She chuckled. "I always do. It's the pills they give me here. I'm talking one minute and out cold the next. But you know, Kathleen, when I sleep, I can see things just like I used to. I can see Harry S., or Peggy. Anybody."

Azzie felt some moisture on one side of her mouth and wiped it away with her hand. "When people are old, Kathleen, they say these sorts of things. I wish you would answer me, Kathy; it upsets me when you don't say anything. Peggy does that and it hurts my . . . but it doesn't matter. I think she must be dead." Azzie covered her wet eyes. "I think he must be dead. I don't know where else he could be, he's been gone for so long. I am a blind stupid old woman." She shook her head back and forth. "I wish to God I could bring him back."

"Mr. Snow."

"I think he is sick."

"What is it?" His tongue felt bloated, unfamiliar.

"But he wanted to go so much."

"What is it?" he tried to shout.

"Your birthday party," a woman answered.

"Who are you?"

"What?"

"Who?"

"Mrs. Newman. Go back to sleep, Mr. Snow." The voice turned away. "Do you think he can have a piece of cake with his dinner?"

Ira stared at his flaccid hands. "What happened?"

"You had a shot early this morning. That is what is making you sleepy. Don't fight it; just go back to sleep."

He tried to raise himself. "A shot!" It sounded distant, like one stranger calling to another more than a block away.

"You had quite an attack." A different woman spoke to him from his left.

"Good night, Mr. Snow. Happy birthday."

"Cake," he said, thinking of Sarah.

"I don't think he should have any cake."

"There must be some little candy that wouldn't hurt." The higher voice returned. "Some punch."

Ira pushed the blanket down over his knees. His pajamas were open and he put his hand to his abdomen. "Please. I must go."

"No. Mr. Snow, you can't go."

He propelled himself to sitting and slid forward, his pajamas falling to the floor as he stood. "Please, I must go." He tried to unwind his pajamas from around his feet. "Help me, please."

Mr. Parker sat next to him, his elbow linked stiffly with Ira's. "I told you these things are a bore. You have no business being here in your condition, hardly able to sit up. You ought to be in bed, taking care of yourself. Taking your pills. Oh, God, look at this. They're going to let Marsh Colloway make a speech."

"Do you see her, Henry?"

"I've been living on this here good earth for eighty years now," Mr. Colloway began. "Eighty-two my wife will tell you, but that's just to make her look young." He guffawed and Henry Parker grimaced.

"Did you hear that? Pompous bastard."

"Long hair, Henry." Ira leaned close to him. "Long black hair. Is she here?"

"Being eighty years old like I am, I don't think I would be bragging or immodest to say that I've learned a lot."

"I'm eighty-seven!" Dorothy Tyler shouted from the back of the room. "Eighty-eight the twenty-ninth of this month."

"Sarah, Henry."

"What are you saying, Ira?"

"Sarah, my friend Sarah." Ira put his hands to his face. "She is coming for my party. Which one is she, Henry? Long hair."

Mr. Parker was staring at him. "She is here, Henry," Ira insisted. "Bring her to me, please!"

"She is not here, Ira," Mr. Parker answered and watched Ira bite his finger. "There is no one young here."

Ira looked around desperately.

"I am going to take you back to the room. No, Ira, don't argue about it." Mr. Parker pulled Ira from his chair by his arms, Ira's face falling on his shoulder. "Cake." Ira spoke in his ear. "She wants cake, Henry. Bring cake."

CHAPTER 20

From: Ima M. Johnston
Twilight Days Rest Home

To: *Mr. Jamie Throckmorton*
  Next of kin to Kathleen B. Storrs

December 18, 1956

Mr. Throckmorton,

I am sorry to inform you that as of this day, your cousin's condition has deteriorated to the extent that I am no longer able to care for her in my home. Mrs. Storrs has suffered some sort of stroke or attack, and has not taken solid food for over a week. We have been feeding her three times a day intravenously, but these feedings are quite expensive, and the money the state provides for a charity case is not sufficient to keep this up. I have made the decision to transfer Mrs. Storrs to the state hospital at Valorda, where they have more substantial funds and personnel.

I am enclosing several forms which need your signature. Please send them back to me at your earliest possible convenience.

> *Sincerely,*
> *Ima M. Johnston*

"Is it snowing?" Azzie asked when she heard the door open.

"Snowing?" Henrietta Newman closed the door behind her.

"I can sure feel the cold air when I'm sitting over here."

"No, it isn't snowing. What are you doing in here, Azalea?"

"Kathy asked me to stay," Azzie replied. "Did you see what they brought me?" She held up a pink toothbrush. "They said my teeth smell bad and they gave me this. I don't know why they didn't tell me before. That's one of the things you just don't know by yourself." She touched her face. "Do you remember how my eyes used to be? I used to have such pretty, clear eyes."

"How is Mrs. Storrs doing today?" Henrietta Newman asked abruptly.

Azzie brightened. "I think she seems better this morning. She likes having me here with her."

"How do you know that? She hasn't said anything to you, has she?"

"Sometimes I think she watches me." Azzie's head followed the sound of Mrs. Newman's steps across the room. "She is worn out, you know. People get like that sometimes, and you have to let them sleep it off. I remember one time my daughter said something mean to me; she was just a baby and didn't know any better. But I slept through three days straight. Only woke up once for a glass of water."

Mrs. Newman opened a drawer of Kathleen's bureau. "I wonder where all of her clothes are. Do you know?"

"Her clothes? She's got some of them on, I should

hope. What do you need any more for?" Azzie touched the cold steel arm of her chair.

Mrs. Newman opened the closet door and pulled out a man's brown suitcase. "It feels like somebody's already packed her things. Well, that's fine; save me some trouble."

"What does she need her clothes for?" Azzie tried to stand.

"How is your daughter, Azalea?"

"Which daughter?" The question surprised her and she sat back.

"Which daughter? You only have one as far as I know. The one in Louisiana."

"I don't want to talk about her."

"Oh, really? That's a switch. Suit yourself." She pulled a smaller, green bag from the closet and laid it flat on the floor, next to the brown one, and opened them both to make sure things were in order.

"You're not taking Kathy anywhere? You can't, you know; she needs me. She asked me to stay here with her. You can't take her anywhere." Azzie's voice plummeted. "That's not what you are thinking, is it, because you can't take her anywhere."

Mrs. Newman was surprised by the number of books and papers she found. The brown suitcase was filled with them, and in the smaller, green one was what looked like a hundred letters, all tied in small packets.

"Not very far," she answered without thinking.

"What did you think of them last night?" Vidy plopped down next to Miss Zeagler on a couch in the community room.

Margot Zeagler turned her eyes slowly in Vidy's direction. "Were you addressing me?" she inquired, her fingers playing with their mates.

"Yes, yes. I thought they were big myself."

"Them? I'm sorry, I don't know them."

"They went into your room. I saw them myself. I didn't think it was right"—Vidy washed her chin—"and I said, 'Hey! What are you folks doing?' Didn't you hear me?"

"No. I must have been sleeping. What did they do?"

Vidy studied Miss Zeagler quizzically. "Did you get that orange on your lip from a candy?"

"A candy?" Miss Zeagler's face fled from the scrutiny. "Oh, my goodness, no. I never eat candy."

"Becky done gave me some candy once. Little red piece." Vidy marked the size on her fat thumb. "Hot it was, like tar. Stuck, too." She laughed. "Did she give you any?"

"No." Miss Zeagler stood slowly. "It's time for my nap."

"It burned you, I bet."

"It was very nice to meet you." Miss Zeagler drifted toward the door.

CHAPTER 21

A blue-and-yellow flowered card stared at Ira from the table beside his bed. "To you, Friend, on Your Birthday." The card was from Uncle Robert; Mr. Parker had given him three pairs of dark socks. Best something practical, he had explained while Ira opened the small box. Best something practical when in doubt.

Mr. Parker was talking to Uncle Robert now. Ira lay with his eyes closed, though awake. Two pills were in his ear.

"There weren't any fish in that lake," Henry Parker complained.

"There were," Uncle Robert insisted. "We just hit that stream at the wrong time of year."

"I didn't see a one."

"Of course not. Spring's the time, and we were there in what? October? Remember that cornbread you made for us?" Uncle Robert made a face and they both laughed.

"And that damned armadillo that kept bothering us all night."

"Does Ira know that story?"

Mr. Parker glanced over his shoulder. "I think he is sleeping."

A paper napkin rustled behind Ira's head when he moved. The cake inside was two days old and hardening. Ira was remembering.

"Afternoon."

A faraway wind chime swung wildly. "Afternoon," Ira returned.

"Too cold to sit out here," Andrew Carlyle decided.

"I was watching for someone."

"Listen to that wind!"

"It is my birthday, you know."

"No, I didn't. Happy birthday." Mr. Carlyle opened the front door. "You can count on it. There's going to be a storm tonight."

"You go on to dinner, Henry," Ira told him. "She must be up there having a bite to eat. Probably starved after her trip. Tell her I have some chocolate cake for her, send her down to me. Don't keep her up there talking."

Mr. Parker had been napping. He sat up and rubbed his face. "She's already missed your party, Ira. Are you sure she is coming?"

"Today is my birthday! Not Friday. Sarah hasn't missed anything."

The day seemed prolonged. Uncle Robert and Mr. Parker were still talking. Ira tried to curl his toes around the bottom of the mattress.

"Kathy, Kathy, sit up and put this on." Azzie held open her heavy maroon sweater. "You need something to keep you from catching cold. We have to go outside and it is raining. We have to go to town." She talked as she fumbled with Kathleen's limp arms. "I don't know how far it is, but it can't be too far. Jason walks there every day.

"Is that on you? I can't see; I'm not sure. I know you're tired, Kathy, but you must help me. In town I'm going to call a friend of yours, Mr. Roscoe of Cambria." She pushed Kathleen's spindly legs over the side of the bed. "You know him; he has a car. You can sleep when we get on the road." Azzie shook the loose shoulders. "You must wake up! We have to get out of here. Wake up!"

It was almost time to go. Mr. Parker was sleeping. Ira lay still, thinking of the route to the Gulf station, where the Greyhound made its stop. He would walk down Carolina to Main, where there were some street lamps. With the rain, it would be a difficult walk to make without any light.

What would Sarah bring for his birthday? he wondered. Chocolate turtles, perhaps. Or peppermints. Sarah loved peppermints and would want to share them. He could imagine just how she—

The light seared his eyes. The sound of thick hose rubbing together came close to him. He closed his eyes tightly.

A warm hand lifted his arm. He pulled away.

"Mr. Snow? Are you awake?"

"What?"

"Don't be alarmed. It is Mrs. Crawford. I'm going to give you a little injection."

"No!" He cradled his arm.

"You can go right back to sleep," she promised.

"I've had two pills today. I don't need it."

She made the inside of his elbow wet. "The doctor thought it would be a good idea to have a shot every two nights, just for a few weeks. We don't want you to have another attack. It puts a strain on your heart."

"In the morning," Ira pleaded. "It is my birthday."

"Oh, that's right, it was today, wasn't it? Happy birthday." She slid the needle in and out expertly. "There, it's all over. Good night, Mr. Snow, and happy birthday."

Ira was up before the door closed. He must hurry. He took his pants from the dresser, before the medicine had time to spread. He was excited and dressed himself easily, swiftly.

It was raining harder. Ira inched up the window. A hissing spray shot into the room. He held his breath, but Mr. Parker did not move.

The drop to the ground was uneven. Ira caught himself on his hands, both knees sinking into the mud. He kept himself low and sped across the lawn to the parking lot like a frantic small animal.

Azzie closed the door behind her. "Are you still asleep? I didn't want you to worry. I've been to see Jason. He'll give me anything; I told you he would. I got a letter from my daughter, did I tell you? It was quite some time ago, but I believe that I failed to mention it." Azzie sat down heavily on the edge of the bed and Kathleen stirred. "She has moved. She doesn't live in Louisiana anymore. Someplace in Oklahoma where they don't have a hospital.

"I wonder if Peggy took her husband with her." She turned the book of matches over in her hand. "I think she got rid of him somewhere along the way. He was French, you must know that; that's where she got her name, Poteat. I always thought it was a pretty name. I told her that the night she told me she was getting married. She was only seventeen; I reminded her of that. But, I said, you are getting a fine name that you can use all of your life. Peggy Poteat. People will think you are somebody."

Azzie opened the cardboard cover. "I can see these, did you know that? I can see all kinds of light, and a few colors. Orange, purple. That's all. She moved, though, Peggy. She doesn't live in Louisiana anymore. I wanted to tell you; I didn't want to leave you thinking that I was still going off to have that operation." Azzie raised her voice. "Because I'm not."

She felt for a corner of the bed sheet. "I've done a terrible thing, Kathy. I've told you that, I've apologized. But it could be much worse." She struck a match, the flame warming her palm. "If I could see, we could think of another way." Azzie held the match to the corner of the sheet for an instant, dropping it when the heat came too near. "If only they had taken me for my operation, I could take care of you." She lit another match and studied the light. "But they've left me without my eyes."

It was twenty minutes until eleven. In room 9B, Elizabeth Colloway sat up in bed and spat out a mustard phlegm. Her husband spoke to her in half sleep. "Get it all out, Lizzie." Emit Street in the next room heard the noise and rolled over, sending his pillow to the floor.

Fronie MacDermott had left Dorothy Tyler an hour earlier, and Mrs. Tyler was just slipping into sleep. The table beside her still displayed the results of the last hand of gin. In the next bed, Jimi June slept soundly, her orange-and-black cat pressed to her belly, the ring under her palm.

Vidy was quietly singing a Christmas song she had learned last Friday in Sunday school. Becky Springer sat in a chair, listening to the rain and thinking of her garden. Her head nodded; the low hum of Vidy's carol was lulling her to sleep.

Max Churcher rubbed his stomach sleepily. Earl Brogdon was sleeping deeply.

"I've been thinking, Cranson, that we ought to ring up Jane Beth before too long. Edna would like that; it's one of the things she asked for specially. But you're going to have to behave yourself. Anyway, Jane Beth's not so bad. Invite her up for a Sunday. She'd probably bring something, and we wouldn't mind that, would we? Somebody brought old Henry a cake the other day, and that got me to thinking."

Mrs. Crawford was napping on the cot she had made for herself in the laundry room. Henry Parker dreamed of a trip he had taken to Missouri. Three rooms down the hall, Margot Zeagler slept with her hip raised, the linen of her bed stained with apricot lip rouge. No one was watching the lights of the Christmas tree. Red, green, yellow, blue flashed on the ceiling. From the table the paper Santa winked, his black-mittened hand raised in perpetual greeting.